"You Think People Will Believe I'm Carrying Your Baby?"

Sheldon moved closer to where Renee stood. "I'm certain some people will believe that."

"Oh, Sheldon, what are we going to do?"

"You could let me take care of you," Sheldon said without hesitation.

Renee's mind spun in bewilderment. "What exactly are you saying?"

"You could live with me and be my hostess."

Renee's emotions churned out of control as she tried to make sense of his proposition.

"But you're my boss," she said, shaking her head in confusion. "Are you proposing some sort of business arrangement?"

Sheldon studied Renee thoughtfully for a moment. "And if I weren't your boss?"

Tilting her chin defiantly, Renee gave Sheldon a challenging look. "You didn't answer my question, Mr. Blackstone. Would our arrangement be for business or pleasure?"

Sheldon leaned close to her, close enough for his breath to caress her cheek. "That decision would be up to you, Miss Wilson."

Dear Reader,

Thank you for choosing Silhouette Desire. As always, we have a fabulous array of stories for you to enjoy, starting with *Just a Taste* by Bronwyn Jameson, the latest installment in our DYNASTIES: THE ASHTONS continuity series. This tale of forbidden attraction between two romance-wary souls will leave you breathless and wanting more from this wonderful author—who will have a brand-new miniseries of her own, PRINCES OF THE OUTBACK, out later this year.

The terrific Annette Broadrick is back with another book in her CRENSHAWS OF TEXAS series. *Double Identity* is an engrossing page-turner about seduction and lies…you know, all that good stuff! Susan Crosby continues her BEHIND CLOSED DOORS series with *Rules of Attraction*, the first of three brand-new stories set in the world of very private investigations. Roxanne St. Claire brings us a fabulous McGrath brother hero caught in an unexpected situation, in *When the Earth Moves*. Rochelle Alers's THE BLACKSTONES OF VIRGINIA series wraps up with *Beyond Business*, a story in which the Blackstone patriarch gets involved in a surprise romance with his new—and very pregnant—assistant. And last but certainly not least, the engaging Amy Jo Cousins is back this month with *Sleeping Arrangements*, a terms-of-the-will story not to be missed.

Here's hoping you enjoy all six of our selections this month. And, in the months to come, look for Maureen Child's THREE-WAY WAGER series and a brand-new installment of our infamous TEXAS CATTLEMAN'S CLUB.

Happy reading!

Melissa Jeglinski

Melissa Jeglinski
Senior Editor
Silhouette Desire

Beyond Business

ROCHELLE ALERS

Published by Silhouette Books
America's Publisher of Contemporary Romance

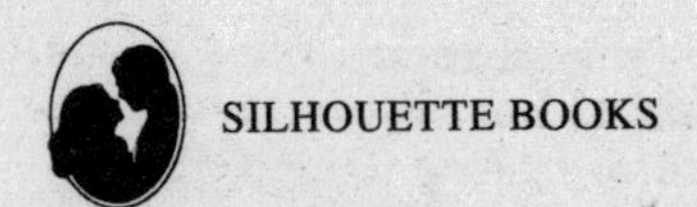

ISBN 0-373-76649-1

BEYOND BUSINESS

This edition published by arrangement with Harlequin Books S.A.

Visit Silhouette Books at www.eHarlequin.com

Printed in U.S.A.

Books by Rochelle Alers

Silhouette Desire

A Younger Man #1479
**The Long Hot Summer* #1565
**Very Private Duty* #1613
**Beyond Business* #1649

*The Blackstones of Virginia

ROCHELLE ALERS

is a native New Yorker who lives on Long Island. She admits to being a hopeless romantic, who is in love with life. Rochelle's hobbies include traveling, music, art and preparing gourmet dinners for friends and family members. A cofounder of Women Writers of Color, Rochelle was the first proud recipient of the Vivian Stephens Career Achievement Award for Excellence in Romance Novel Writing. You can contact her at P.O. Box 690, Freeport, NY 11520-0690, or roclers@aol.com.

Dedicated to Oliver Lewis—
the first jockey of any race to win the Kentucky Derby.

The children of those who serve you will dwell secure,
and their descendants live on in your presence.
—*Psalms* 102:28

One

"Please state your name," came the computer-generated voice through a speaker mounted on a post. A pair of electronic iron gates emblazoned with a bold letter *B* and closed-circuit cameras marked the entrance to the fabled Blackstone Farms.

Leaning out the driver's side window, Renee stared up at the camera. "Renee Wilson." Within seconds the gates opened and then closed behind her as she drove through.

New state, new job and a new beginning, she mused, driving past acres of white rail fences, stone walls and verdant landscaped grassland.

She smiled and returned the wave from a man sitting atop a tractor hauling bundled hay, sat up straighter and rolled her head from side to side. She was stiff—neck, shoulders and lower back. She'd made the trip from Louisville, Kentucky, to Staunton, Virginia, in a little more than eight hours, stopping only twice to refuel her car and eat.

"Yes," she whispered softly. She *had* made the right decision to accept the position as the administrative assistant for Blackstone Farms. Living and working on a horse farm would be a new experience for someone accustomed to the pulsating kinetic energy of Miami. And as much as she loved the south Florida city, with its personality and colorful residents, Renee knew she could not have remained there.

She had not wanted to risk running into her ex-lover who'd gotten her pregnant; a man who had conveniently neglected to tell her that he was married, she thought bitterly.

Slowing at a section where the road diverged into four directions, she followed the sign pointing the way to the main house. A towering flagpole with the American flag flying atop a black-and-red one lifted in the slight breeze.

It was late October, and trees were displaying their vibrant fall colors. The odor of wet earth lingered in the crisp autumn air from a week of thunderstorms that had left the Appalachian and Shenandoah Mountain regions saturated and lush.

Renee maneuvered her sedan behind a pickup truck in the driveway leading to Sheldon Blackstone's house. She had been interviewed and hired by his son Jeremy, who would eventually become her boss upon his father's retirement at the end of the year.

She turned off the engine, scooped her handbag off the passenger seat and pushed open the door. Her shoes had barely touched the ground when a tall figure loomed in front of her. Startled, she let out a soft gasp at the same time her head jerked up.

A pair of light gray eyes under curving black eyebrows in a deeply tanned olive-brown face pinned her to the spot. The afternoon sunlight glinted off streaks of red and flecks of gray in a full head of black wavy hair. Her breathing halted, her heart pounded erratically and a lack of oxygen made her feel light-headed. There was no doubt he was Sheldon. The resemblance between father and son was uncanny. But there was something in the elder Blackstone's gaze that unnerved her.

Recovering and letting out a soft exhalation of breath, she extended a hand. "Good afternoon. I'm Renee Wilson."

Sheldon Blackstone stared at the small hand before he shook it, her fingers disappearing in his larger grasp. He wondered how the woman with the delicate features in a nut-brown face and blunt-cut, chin-length hairdo would react once he informed her that she would have to live with him instead of in the bungalow she had been assigned.

Sheldon forced a smile he did not feel. "Sheldon Blackstone."

Renee eased her hand from his firm grip. "My pleasure, Mr. Blackstone."

Sheldon angled his head while raising an eyebrow. "Please call me Sheldon. Around here we're very informal."

The smile softening Renee's lush mouth deepened the dimples in her cheeks. "Then Sheldon it is, but only if you call me Renee."

His smile became a full grin. He found her dimpled smile enchanting. "Renee it is." Cupping her elbow, he led her toward the large two-story white house trimmed in black with an expansive wraparound porch. "I have something to tell you before you settle in."

Renee glanced at his distinctive profile. High slanting cheekbones, an aquiline nose, penetrating light gray eyes and a square-cut jaw made for an arresting visage. She stopped on the first step. "Jeremy told me everything about the position during the interview, including my duties and benefits."

Sheldon turned and stared down at her. "It's about your housing."

Renee closed her eyes for several seconds. She prayed the Blackstones would not renege on their promise to provide her with resident housing or on-site child care.

"What about it?"

Sheldon crossed his arms over his broad chest. "The bungalow assigned to you is uninhabitable. Unfortunately, lightning struck the roof, setting it afire. After we put the fire out, it rained. I had a contractor assess the damage yesterday, and he said he'll have to gut it before it can be renovated."

Renee's eyes widened with this disclosure as she curbed the urge to bite down on her lower lip as she usually did when upset or frustrated. "Are you saying I can't live *here*?"

Sheldon dropped his arms and reached for her elbow again. "Let's go inside and discuss your options."

She froze, her eyes widening again. She only had one option—if she couldn't live at Blackstone Farms she'd have to get into her car and drive back to Kentucky. And while Sheldon Blackstone wanted to discuss housing options she wanted to tell him that she was a thirty-five-year-old single woman, without a permanent residence *and* pregnant with the child of a lying man who had reconciled with his wife.

"Please, Renee, hear me out. Let's go into the house," Sheldon said in a deep, quiet voice.

She stared at him for several seconds before nodding. "Okay, Sheldon."

Renee would listen to what he had to say, but felt uneasy. Why, she asked herself, couldn't she find a man she could trust; they say one thing and do the complete opposite. It had begun with her father. Errol

Wilson had been an alcoholic, liar, gambler and a philanderer.

She dated from time to time, and although she had offered a few men her passion, she refused to give any her love. But everything had changed when she met Donald Rush. She offered him everything she'd withheld from every other man, and in the end he, too, had deceived her. With the others she had been able to walk away unscathed with her pride and dignity intact, but her luck had run out. It wasn't until after she'd moved out of Donald's house and spent two months with her brother and his family that she discovered she was pregnant with a married man's child.

Renee followed Sheldon up the porch and into the house. An expansive entryway was crowded with a breakfront and beveled glass curio cabinets. Many of the shelves were filled with trophies, mementoes and faded photographs of black jockeys from the mid-nineteenth century to the present. She walked through a formal living room and into another large room with a leather seating arrangement. Streams of sunlight poured in through mullioned floor-to-ceiling windows.

Sheldon pointed to a club chair. "Please sit down." He waited for Renee to sit before taking a matching love seat several feet away. He crossed one denim-covered knee over the other. He didn't know what it was, but something told him that the woman Jeremy had interviewed and subsequently hired to computerize the farm's business records would not make it through her three-month probationary period. He'd read her résumé and although she'd been office manager for one of the most prestigious law firms in Miami, it did not compare to living and working on a horse farm. He wondered how long would it take for her to tire of smelling hay and horseflesh.

He doubted whether he would have hired Renee despite her experience and exemplary references, but that decision had been taken out of his hands. She would eventually become Jeremy's responsibility once he assumed complete control of running Blackstone Farms. The final transfer of thirty years of power would take effect January first.

His gaze moved slowly from her professionally coiffed hair to a yellow silk tunic, and down to a pair of black wool crepe slacks and leather slip-ons with a renowned designer's logo. Everything about Renee Wilson screamed big-city sophistication.

"As I said before you won't be able to live in your bungalow for a few months," Sheldon began in a quiet tone. "However, I'm prepared to open my home to you until the repairs are completed."

Renee sat forward on her chair. "I'll be living with you?" She'd vowed never to live with another man, even temporarily; but she also had to remind herself that Sheldon Blackstone would be her boss for the next two months, not her lover.

The beginnings of a smile crinkled Sheldon's

eyes. There was no doubt his suggestion had shocked her. "This is a big house. We won't be bumping into each other. I have a housekeeper who comes in several times a week to clean and do laundry. You'll have your own bedroom with a private bath, and a makeshift office has been set up for you on the back porch. If you don't want to take your meals in the main dining hall, or have them delivered, you may use the kitchen. If you prefer cooking for yourself, just let me know what you'll need and I'll order it from the head chef."

Despite her consternation, Renee affected a smile. "It seems as if you've thought of everything." Sheldon, flashing a rare, open smile, nodded. "My living here with you won't pose a problem for your…" Her words trailed off.

Sheldon uncrossed his legs, clasped his hands together and planted his booted feet firmly on the parquet floor. "Are you referring to another woman?" Renee's averted gaze answered his question. "That will not be a problem for either of us," he continued. "There are two Mrs. Blackstones—my sons' wives, Kelly and Tricia." Her head came up. "My wife died twenty years ago, and I've never been involved with *any* woman who either lived or worked on this farm."

Renee let out an inaudible sigh. "Well then, I'll accept your offer."

Sheldon hadn't lied to Renee. There were no other women in his life, hadn't been in months. He had married at seventeen, become a father at eighteen, was widowed at thirty-two and now at fifty-three he planned to retire at the end of the year.

His retirement plans included fishing, traveling and spoiling his grandchildren. He wasn't actively seeking a woman to share his life, but if one did come along who shared similar interests, then he would consider a more permanent relationship—a relationship that was certain not to include marriage. He'd failed once as a husband and didn't want to repeat it.

He hadn't lived a monkish existence since burying his wife, but at no time had he ever advertised his liaisons. All of his encounters were always conducted off the farm. No one, and that included his sons, knew any of the women who shared his bed after he'd become a widower.

"There is a slight problem," Renee said as Sheldon pushed to his feet."

"What's that?"

"I've ordered furniture and it's scheduled to be delivered here today."

"It arrived earlier this morning," he informed her, "and I took the responsibility of having everything stored at a warehouse in Richmond."

Renee sighed in relief and rose to her feet. "Thank you."

She'd sold the entire contents of her Miami condominium before moving into Donald's palatial

Miami Beach oceanfront home, and the day she left him she'd walked away with only her clothes and personal items.

Sheldon smiled at the petite woman whose head came to his shoulder. "Let me show you to your room."

"I need to get my luggage from my car."

He extended his hand. "Give me your key and I'll get it."

Opening her handbag, Renee handed him the key. A slight shock rippled up her arm as her fingers made contact with Sheldon's. She stared up at him to see if he'd felt the same reaction, but his expression was reserved.

Slipping the key into the pocket of his jeans, Sheldon escorted Renee to a curving staircase leading to the second floor. Her fingertips trailed over the mahogany banister. Their footsteps were muffled in the carpeted hallway.

Sheldon walked past three bedrooms, stopping at the last one on the right. "This one is yours. It has its own sitting room and private bath."

Renee moved beyond Sheldon and into a large, sun-filled space, feeling as if she had stepped back in time. A massive mirrored pale green armoire, the only color in the near-white bedroom, was the room's focal point. An elegant antique, white, queen-size iron bed provided the perfect complement for the armoire.

She made her way to a door in a far corner. A bathroom with an old-fashioned claw-foot bathtub, yellow floral wallpaper dotted with sprigs of leaves and berries picked up the pale green hues of an upholstered chair in a corner. Antique wall sconces added the perfect finishing touch. She left the bathroom and reentered the bedroom, noting that the bathroom's wallpaper was repeated in the sitting room.

She smiled at Sheldon as he rested a shoulder against the open door, arms crossed over his chest. His pose reminded her of a large lounging cat. "It's perfect."

He flashed an open smile. He'd thought Renee would consider the bedroom too old-fashioned. After all, she had lived in one of the country's most cosmopolitan southern cities.

He straightened from his leaning position. "I'll bring up your luggage." He turned to leave, then stopped. "Would you like something to eat or drink? Just for tonight, dinner will be served an hour later than usual."

Renee glanced at her watch. It was after four, and she was scheduled to eat again at six. Her obstetrician had recommended she eat five small meals instead of three big ones. She had just begun her second trimester, and she had gained an average of two pounds each month.

"What time is dinner?"

"Tonight it will begin at seven."

There was no way she would be able to wait three hours before eating again, not unless she wanted a pounding headache or a fainting spell.

"I'd like a fruit salad and a glass of milk."

Sheldon's expression stilled and grew serious. "Are you a health-food fanatic?"

Renee flashed a bright smile. "I decided a couple of months ago to eat healthy. No fast foods, gooey snacks or anything with additives or preservatives."

Light gray eyes studied her intently. "Perhaps you living with me will help me reconsider some of my dietary choices." His only weakness was ice cream—lots of ice cream.

"You look quite fit to me." The words were out of Renee's mouth before she could censor herself.

Sheldon gave her a direct stare. His last physical indicated he was in excellent health for a man his age. He stood six-one and weighed one-ninety, and with a break in the hot weather he'd begun the practice of leaving his truck in the driveway and walking more.

Sheldon and Renee regarded each other with a waiting that hadn't been there before. Again, Renee felt uneasy, as if she were a specimen under a powerful microscope. She did not know the owner of Blackstone Farms and she did not want to come to know him—at least not beyond an employer-employee relationship.

She would live in Sheldon's house until her bungalow was habitable, organize and computerize years of paperwork that had been done manually and come spring she hoped to deliver a healthy son or daughter. She refused to plan beyond the time her child would go from the farm's infant center to its preschool and subsequently to the day school.

Sheldon blinked as if coming out of a trance. "I'd better go and get your bags."

His deep, soothing voice shattered the silence between them, and Renee nodded in agreement. She stood in the same spot until pressure on her bladder forced her to retreat to the bathroom.

When she returned to the bedroom she spied her bags. Two sat on the floor next to a closet, while the largest rested on a whitewashed wooden bench at the foot of the bed. Sheldon had carried up all three bags in one trip where it would have taken her at least two, maybe three.

There was no doubt he was physically fit; he was tall, broad-shouldered with a trim waist and hips. It was the first time she'd encountered a man whose magnificent physique matched his face. Sheldon Blackstone was drop-dead gorgeous.

Slipping off her shoes, she decided to shower before eating. She would have to forego what had become a regularly scheduled afternoon nap. There were times when she'd felt so exhausted that she could not keep her eyes open, but thank goodness up till now she hadn't experienced morning sickness.

The reality that she was to become a mother had changed her outlook on life. Everything she did and every decision she made was predicated on the tiny life growing inside her.

There had been a time when she was forced to give up her dream to graduate from law school. After her father drank himself into an early grave, she went to work to help supplement her mother's meager income. But her dream of graduating college was delayed for more than a decade. It had taken her six years as a part-time student, but she did it. She now held a degree in pre-law.

Renee closed her eyes and smiled. *Live for today, and let tomorrow take care of itself.* That had been her mother's mantra, and it was now hers.

Two

Sheldon drove past the area where a large white tent had been erected for the evening's pre-race festivities. Dozens of tables were covered in white linen; folding chairs, swathed white organza tied with either black or red satin ribbon, represented the farm's silks.

It had been several years since Blackstone Farms had hosted a pre-race gala. This year was different because Ryan and Jeremy had decided to enter Shah Jahan in the International Gold Cup race.

The thoroughbred had become the farm's racing secret, along with its jockey. Seeing diminutive Cheryl Carney astride the magnificent black colt never failed to make Sheldon's heart stop whenever horse and rider crossed the finish line. Cheryl's uncle and head trainer, Kevin Manning, had clocked Jahan at one minute, fifty-nine and one-fifth seconds for a mile and a quarter—the distance run by three-year-olds in the Kentucky Derby. The record was one-fifth second faster than Secretariat's fastest winning time in Derby history.

Sheldon took a right turn and headed for the stables. He maneuvered into a space between his sons' SUVs. He left his truck and walked into the veterinarian's office.

"Isn't it a little early for celebrating?" he asked at the same time Ryan and Jeremy touched glasses filled with an amber liquid.

Dr. Ryan Blackstone smiled at his father. He lifted his glass. "Not early enough. Jeremy has good news for you."

Jeremy shifted on his chair and smiled at his father. "Tricia and I just got back from the doctor. She's pregnant."

Sheldon's smile matched his youngest son's. He pumped his fist in the air and howled, "Boo-yaw! Give me some of that sissy stuff you're about to drink. Once you come over to my place I'll give you a shot of my special blend."

"No, Pop!"

"Oh, hell no."

Jeremy and Ryan had protested in unison.

"I know someone at ATF whom I'm certain would

like to test your so-called special blend," Jeremy teased with a wide grin.

Frowning, Sheldon shook his head. "I can't believe my boys have gone soft on me."

Ryan reached for the bottle of bourbon in a cabinet behind his desk and poured a small amount into a glass for Sheldon. His dark gray eyes crinkled in amusement. "You can keep that special blend. I'd rather drink something that doesn't double as paint thinner or drain cleaner."

Sheldon's expression softened. He was proud of Jeremy and Ryan. It hadn't been easy trying to raise his two adolescent boys after Julia died. That time had been a low point in his life because he'd worked around the clock to keep the horse farm solvent while attempting to provide emotional support for his grieving children.

Ryan had become a veterinarian. He'd returned to the farm to start his practice. It had taken Jeremy fourteen years, a four-year stint in the Marine Corps and a brief career as a special agent for the Drug Enforcement Administration before he'd settled down on the farm. After recuperating from an injury he'd sustained several months before during an undercover mission in South America, Jeremy had reconnected with his childhood sweetheart, Tricia Parker. Now he and Tricia would give Sheldon his third grandchild.

The three men touched glasses. Ryan and Jeremy

took furtive sips while Sheldon tossed back his drink in one swallow. He set the glass down on the desk.

"Next time buy something that doesn't taste like Kool-Aid."

Ryan frowned from under lowered lids. "There's nothing wrong with this bourbon."

Sheldon rolled his eyes at Ryan and straddled a corner of the large desk. "Renee Wilson arrived about an hour ago," he said without preamble.

Jeremy sat up straighter. "How did she take the news that she would have to live with you until her place is renovated?"

Sheldon shrugged a shoulder, the gesture quite elegant for a man his size. "I suspect she wasn't too happy about it, but she didn't show it."

Leaning back in his chair, Ryan propped his booted feet on his desk and stared directly at his father. "Jeremy told me you cussed a blue streak when he suggested she live with you."

Sheldon glared at Jeremy. "You talk too much."

Jeremy returned the glare. "Well, you did, Pop. You said words I hadn't heard since Ryan and I were kids." There had been a time when he'd used foul language because he'd heard his father use it. He paid for the infractions whenever his mother washed his mouth with lye soap. But that ended once Julia Blackstone passed away. Jeremy stopped cursing and Sheldon stopped talking. Days would go by before he would utter a single word.

"Would you like to hear a few more?" Sheldon asked.

Jeremy held up a hand and shook his head. "No, thank you. What do you think of Renee?"

"If you're asking me whether she's qualified for the job, only time will tell."

A flash of humor glinted in Jeremy's smoky gray eyes. "Personally I think she's rather cute."

Sheldon gave his youngest son an incredulous stare. "Is that why you hired her? Because she's cute?"

Jeremy sobered quickly. "No. I hired her because she's qualified. In fact, her skills are exceptional. So much so that I wonder why she'd leave a position where she earned twice what we are going to pay her to live on a horse farm."

"Only time will tell," Sheldon responded. *Perhaps she's hiding from something or someone,* he added silently. "Is Jahan ready for tomorrow?" he asked, deftly changing the topic.

He did not want to think about Renee Wilson, because like Jeremy, he, too, found her cute—very cute and quite sexy. The last woman he'd found that cute and sexy he'd married....

"He's as ready as he will ever be," Ryan answered, bringing Sheldon's thoughts back to the present. "Cheryl had him on the track with three other horses a little while ago, and for the first time he didn't seem so skittish around them. In fact he was very calm once he was led into the gate."

Sheldon stood up. "Make certain Kevin knows he's not to race him without blinkers." Kevin Manning had been Blackstone Farms' head trainer for the past fifteen years.

"We have everything under control, Pop," Ryan said curtly.

Sheldon recognized the thread of irritation creeping into Ryan's voice. Ryan thought he was being controlling again. "I'm going back to the house to get ready. I'll see you later." Leaning over, he patted Jeremy's shoulder. "Congratulations, son."

Jeremy raised his glass in a salute. "Thanks, Pop."

Sheldon glanced at his watch as he climbed the porch steps. He had an hour to ready himself before the residents from neighboring farms arrived for the social event that usually preceded a premier race.

He walked into the house, and felt her presence immediately. It had been a long time, since Jeremy and Ryan moved into their own homes less than a quarter of a mile away, since he'd shared his roof with another person.

He headed for the staircase, but then hesitated when he heard voices. Retracing his steps he walked towards the rear of the house. A slow smile softened his mouth. Renee lay sprawled on a chaise, asleep. A pair of blue sweatpants and an oversized T-shirt had replaced her tailored attire. The radio on a table blared a popular love song.

Soft lighting from a floor lamp flattered her delicate features. Sheldon moved closer until he stood directly over Renee. Her face, relaxed in sleep, appeared so peaceful, angelic.

Who are you? Why are you here? The two questions came to his mind unbidden.

He reached out and touched her shoulder. Her eyes opened and she came awake immediately. Her gaze widened until he could see the dark centers in a pair of heavily lashed eyes that were the color of rich golden sherry. Why hadn't he noticed their odd color before?

Smiling, Sheldon straightened. "I'm sorry to wake you, but you need to get ready for tonight's party."

Renee sat up and combed her fingers through her mussed hair. "What party?"

The lingering effects of sleep had lowered her voice until it was a velvety purr. Why, he asked himself again, hadn't he also noticed the sultriness of her voice? But he knew the answer even before his mind had formed the questions. It was because he did not want to be reminded that he missed female companionship. He had become so accustomed to living alone that he'd let loose with a string of virulent expletives he hadn't uttered in years the moment Jeremy suggested their new employee live with him until her bungalow was repaired.

"Blackstone Farms is hosting a pre-race party.

One of our thoroughbreds will be racing for the first time tomorrow afternoon."

Renee swung her sock-covered feet to the floor. "How often do you host these parties?"

"It's been two years since we hosted the last one. But if Jahan wins, then we'll hold a post-race celebration Sunday afternoon."

She stood up. "Do you expect him to win?"

"There is no doubt he'll win, although the odds are 12-to-1 against him."

"I know nothing about betting on horses."

"Don't worry, I'll show you."

She shook her head. "That's okay. I'd rather not."

"Are you opposed to gambling?"

Renee gave Sheldon a long, penetrating stare. A momentary look of discomfort crossed her face and filled her eyes. "Yes, because my father was an alcoholic and a gambler. A very lethal combination. He had a wife and children who needed his support."

The moment Renee had mentioned her father she was unable to conceal her vulnerability, and Sheldon's protective instincts surfaced without warning. He wanted to take her in his arms and hold her until her pain eased. However, he would not act on his impulse, because he doubted whether she would accept the gesture.

"There's nothing wrong with gambling or drinking, if done in moderation," he countered gently.

"Moderation wasn't in my father's vocabulary."

"You don't gamble or drink." His question was a statement.

"I drink occasionally."

Sheldon smiled. "If Shah Jahan wins tomorrow, will you share a glass of champagne with me?"

Renee shook her head. "I can't."

He sobered. "You can't or you won't?"

"I can't," she repeated.

"Does it have anything to do with you working for me?"

It should only be that easy, Renee thought. She hadn't disclosed her physical condition to Jeremy during her interview, yet knew it was only a matter of time before her pregnancy became evident.

"It has nothing to do with our employee-employer status." He raised a questioning eyebrow once she paused. "I am going to have a baby."

Her explanation hit Sheldon in the face with the force of a stone propelled from a slingshot. "You're pregnant?"

She nodded. "I've just begun my fourth month."

His gaze swept over her chest before dropping to her belly as if he could see under the cotton fabric to see her expanding waistline. "What about your husband?" The farm's employment application had been revised to exclude age and marital status.

Renee was hard-pressed not to laugh at Sheldon's shocked expression. "I'm not married. My baby's father was already married."

"You slept with a married man?" he asked, his tone coolly disapproving.

Pulling back her shoulders, Renee faced him down. "I didn't know he was married. Not until I came home early from a business trip and found a woman in my bed with the man whom I thought I would eventually marry."

A myriad of emotions crossed Sheldon's handsome face. "Does he know about the baby?"

"No." The single word was emphatic.

"Are you going to tell him?"

"No," she repeated.

"He has a right to know that you're carrying his child."

Renee took a step closer to Sheldon, close enough to detect the lingering scent of his aftershave, close enough to see the stubble of an emerging beard on his angular jaw.

"That's where you're wrong. He forfeited that right when he conveniently neglected to tell me he'd married a Las Vegas showgirl when he'd attended a trade show convention there. I'd left Florida before I knew I was pregnant, and I have no intention of returning or contacting him. I don't need him for child support, so that lets him off the hook financially."

Sheldon saw a different woman than the one who had stepped out of her car only a few hours before. Under the delicate exterior was an inner strength that was not apparent at first glance.

She had come to Blackstone Farms to work and live, yet had not come alone. Now he understood why she sought out a position that offered on-site child care. A knowing smile touched his mobile mouth as he recalled the number of babies born to longtime employees who were now a part of the farm's extended family. His daughter-in-law Tricia had been a Blackstone Farms baby.

"I'll call the contractor Monday and have him add another bedroom to your bungalow."

Renee looked at Sheldon in astonishment, her jaw dropping. "Why?" The query came out in a breathless whisper.

Her reaction to his offer amused Sheldon. "Every child needs his or her own room, a place to call their own."

A dimpled smile curved her lush mouth. "You're right. Thank you, Sheldon."

He gave her a direct stare. "Your thanks may be a little premature, because I'm a hard taskmaster, Renee. You'll only have three months to bring Blackstone Farms into the twenty-first century. Everything, and that includes payroll and purchase orders, has been done manually for thirty years. And that translates into thousands of pieces of paper. Jeremy wants the farm's revenue and expenses computerized before he takes over in January.

"If you need someone to assist you on a temporary basis, just ask. More importantly, if you don't understand something, ask questions." His expression softened, his gaze as tender as a caress. "I may bark a lot, but I've never been known to bite."

Within minutes Renee recognized a maddening hint of arrogance in the owner of Blackstone Farms, but there was something in his manner that soothed rather than agitated her. There was no doubt they would be able to live and work together.

"I'll make certain to remember that."

He smiled again. "Good. Now, if you'll excuse me I have to get ready for a party."

She returned his smile. "I'll be ready by seven."

Renee still saw the broad shoulders under a pale blue denim shirt as she leaned over to turn off the radio. The enclosed back porch was the ideal workspace. Screened-in floor-to-ceiling windows faced the southeast. There would be an abundance of light during daylight hours. The area where she sat on the chaise had a wrought-iron table with seating for two, an entertainment center and an adjoining half bath. She could work, eat and relax without leaving the porch.

She would take the weekend to settle in, acquaint herself with the layout of the farm and its residents, before she began the task she'd been hired to do Monday morning.

Nightfall had descended on Blackstone Farms like a translucent navy-blue veil when Sheldon stepped out onto the porch to find Renee sitting on the rocker waiting for him.

His eyes widened in appreciation as she rose gracefully to her feet. She had pinned her hair atop her head, adding several inches, and a pair of three-inch black pumps added further to her diminutive height. A black dress and matching jacket pulled her winning look together. A pair of magnificent diamond earrings adorning her lobes supported Renee's claim that she could support her child on her own.

Sheldon forced himself to concentrate on her face and not her legs. A light breeze stirred the perfume on her body, and he froze. The fragrance had been Julia's favorite.

Renee saw his startled look. "Is something wrong?"

"No," he said a little too quickly. "You look very nice."

A wave of heat washed over her face, settling in her cheeks. "Thank you. So do you." Sheldon's dark suit looked as if it had been tailored expressly for his tall frame.

He moved closer, extending his arm, and he was not disappointed when Renee curved a hand over the sleeve of his suit jacket. "Thank you very much."

Renee was certain Sheldon could feel her trembling. There was something about the man that disturbed her—in every way, and she knew an attraction to him would be perilous to her emotional well-being. She hadn't missed the smoldering flame of awareness in the gray orbs when he'd stepped out onto the porch. The flame had flared to life before he'd successfully shuttered his gaze.

Sheldon looked good, smelled good and felt even better. Her hand rested lightly on his sleeve, yet she felt the power in his arm as hard muscle flexed under her light touch.

"Aren't you going to close the inner door?" she asked as he escorted her off the porch.

Sheldon covered her hand with his free one, squeezing her fingers gently. "My door always stays open until I retire for bed. The same goes for everyone who lives on the farm. That is one of the few mandates everyone is expected to follow."

She glanced up at him as he led her to a luxury sedan parked in the driveway behind his pickup truck. "What are the others?"

"One is that you leave the key to your vehicle in the ignition in case it has to be moved in an emergency, and the most important one is all residents must check in with one another during violent weather."

Sheldon opened the passenger side door and she slid onto the leather seat, mentally filing away the mandates. There was no doubt her life on the farm would be vastly different from the one in Miami.

Her mouth went suddenly dry as she watched Sheldon remove his jacket and hang it up on a hook behind his seat. Suddenly everything about him seemed so much larger, broader. He sat down and turned on the ignition and automatic seat restraints lowered over their chests and waists.

Turning his head, Sheldon stared at Renee. "Is the belt too tight for you?"

She met his gaze, the lights from the dashboard illuminating his eyes. "It's fine, thank you."

She was relieved that she had revealed her pregnancy; however, she did not want Sheldon to make allowances for her because of her condition.

Sheldon shifted the car into gear and backed out of the driveway. Within minutes they arrived at the area where tiny white bulbs, strung over fences, around branches of trees and the poles holding up a massive white tent, sparkled like flawless diamonds. He maneuvered into a parking space. Taped music flowed from large speakers set around the party perimeter in anticipation of an evening of dining and dancing under the autumn sky.

Sheldon slipped into his jacket, then came around the car to assist Renee, his right hand going to the small of her back. She stiffened slightly before relaxing her spine against his splayed fingers.

"I want to introduce you to my daughters-in-law before it gets too crowded," he said close to her ear. Lowering his arm, he reached for her hand, holding it gently and protectively in his warm, strong grasp.

Renee followed Sheldon as he led the way across the tent to a table where two women sat laughing hysterically. Sheldon cleared his throat and their heads came up at the same time.

Both were pretty, but the one with dark slanting eyes in an equally dark brown face was stunning. Her short curly hair was cut to complement her exquisite features.

Sheldon released Renee's hand, reached out and gently pulled Tricia Parker-Blackstone from her chair. Lowering his head, he kissed her cheek. "Congratulations. I'm so happy for you and Jeremy."

Smiling broadly, Tricia hugged Sheldon. "Thank you, Pop."

He held her at arm's length. "How are you feeling?"

"Not too bad. The nausea comes and goes."

He noticed the direction of Kelly and Tricia's gazes. Shifting, he extended a hand to Renee. He wasn't disappointed when she placed her hand in his. "Kelly, Tricia, I'd like for you to meet Renee Wilson, our new administrative assistant. Renee, these are my daughters, Kelly and Tricia. Kelly is headmistress of Blackstone Farms Day School and Tricia is the school's nurse." The three women exchanged handshakes.

Kelly Blackstone had draped a red silk shawl over a flowing black tank dress. She smiled at Renee. "It looks as if you came on board at the right time. Blackstone Farms is renowned for hosting the best pre-race party in Virginia's horse country."

The words were barely off Kelly's lips when a booming voice sliced the night. "Hey, Blackstone! I heard that you have a wonder horse better than the legendary Affirmed." A tall, florid-faced man with tousled silver-blond hair nodded to Tricia and Kelly. "Ladies."

Renee watched Sheldon's expression change, become somber. It was obvious he wasn't too fond of the middle-aged man.

"Someone has been lying to you, Taylor," Sheldon said quietly. "I'm certain you've seen the odds."

Kent Taylor, owner of Taylor Stables, stared boldly at Renee. "That's only because no one outside Blackstone Farms has seen him run."

"You'll see all you'll need to see tomorrow afternoon," Sheldon countered.

When it was obvious Sheldon wasn't going to introduce Renee, Kent Taylor's too-bright grin faded. "Are you saying I should put some money on Shah Jahan?"

"No, I am not." Sheldon's voice was a dangerously soft tone, his southern drawl even more pronounced. "I suggest you bet on something that is a sure thing."

Kent sobered. "Now that sounds like a challenge to me."

A mocking smile crinkled Sheldon's eyes. "That's why we have horse races, Taylor."

Kent nodded in agreement. "Tonight I'm going to enjoy your food and liquor. Sunday afternoon I'll return the favor when I host the post-race victory celebration."

Sheldon's face was marked with loathing as his closest neighbor turned and walked away with an exaggerated swagger. He did not know why the man always attempted to turn the sport of horse-racing into a back-alley brawl.

Kelly grunted softly under her breath. "Now I see why he's been married so many times. No normal woman would be able to tolerate his overblown ego for more than a week."

Tricia waved a hand in front of her face. "He smells as if he's been sampling his own liquor cabinet before he got here."

Within minutes of Kent Taylor's departure Ryan and Jeremy arrived, carrying plates for their wives.

"Taylor just passed us, talking trash as usual," Ryan said, as he set a plate on the table in front of Kelly.

"He's a blowhard," Sheldon spat out.

Jeremy, leaning on a cane, extended his free hand to Renee. "Hello again, and welcome to Blackstone Farms."

She shook his hand before repeating the gesture with Ryan. Sheldon's sons had inherited his dramatic good looks and commanding manner.

Sheldon's arm moved up and around Renee's shoulders. He lowered his head and asked, "Hungry?"

Her head came up, her mouth within inches of his. "Starved."

Smiling, he winked at her. "Good. Come with me."

Renee lay on her side in the darkened bedroom, smiling. She was tired, but too wound up to sleep.

Her first day at Blackstone Farms had become a memorable one. She'd attended her first pre-race party, met people whom she would get to know in the coming weeks and she'd found herself drawn to a man whose roof she would share until her own house was ready to move into.

She closed her eyes, a whisper of a sigh escaping her parted lips. Renee remembered, before sleep claimed her, the power in Sheldon Blackstone's arm whenever it circled her waist. There had been nothing sexual in the gesture, even though his touch communicated comfort and protection: two things she would need in the coming months.

Three

When Renee had gotten up earlier that morning she did not know she would become a participant in a spectacle resembling a fashion show rather than a horse race. She'd called her brother to let him know she had arrived safely, then waited another hour before calling her mother. Her mother had remarried two years before and had relocated to Seattle, Washington, with her new husband and stepchildren.

The weather was picture-perfect for a horse race. A bright blue sky with a few puffy white clouds, temperatures in the midseventies, moderate humidity, no wind and a slightly damp track from an early morning shower set the stage for Virginia's annual International Gold Cup.

She sat in a private box at the Great Meadow racetrack with Sheldon, Ryan, Kelly, Jeremy, Tricia and Kevin Manning, the trainer. Those in the grandstand representing Blackstone Farms had pinned red and black boutonnieres to their lapels.

Renee felt Sheldon's muscled shoulder as she leaned into him. "Why didn't you tell me I'd have to walk the red carpet to get to your box?" Many of the women occupying the private boxes were decked out in haute couture and expensive jewelry.

Sheldon gave Renee a sidelong glance. She had worn her hair down and the ends curved sensuously under her jaw, framing a rounded face that had enraptured him from first glance.

"There was no reason to say anything to you," he said close to her ear. "You have exquisite taste in clothing, and your natural beauty is a refreshing alternative to these plastic women with their designer labels, baubles and surgically altered features and bodies. Some of them have nearly bankrupted their husbands and boyfriends because they view aging as a terminal disease."

Renee did not have time to react to Sheldon's compliment as the voice blaring through the public address system garnered everyone's attention. The horses competing for the International Gold Cup were being led into position at the starting gate.

She peered through a pair of binoculars at the horses. A shiver of excitement coursed through her as she spied Cheryl Carney's petite figure in black-and-red silks atop the magnificent black stallion.

An eerie hush descended over the track as jockeys settled their horses. After several anxiety-filled minutes the gates opened and the horses and riders shot forth.

Renee was on her feet like the others in the box, mouth gaping, heart pounding, legs trembling. Shah Jahan streaked around the track in a blur, his hoofs seemingly never touching the earth. Jeremy and Ryan were shouting at the top of their lungs while Sheldon pounded the railing of the box with both fists. Kevin stood paralyzed, eyes closed, hands fisted, praying silently.

Halfway around the track it was evident the other horses would never catch Shah Jahan. Recovering her voice, Renee screamed along with everyone else. Cheryl and Jahan raced across the finish line eight lengths ahead of the second-place winner, and Renee found herself lifted off her feet and her mouth covered with an explosive kiss that sucked oxygen from her laboring lungs.

Her arms came up of their own volition and curled around Sheldon's neck. She lost herself in the man *and* the moment. Without warning the kiss changed from shared jubilation to a soft, gentle caress and then to an urgent exploration that left her mouth burning with a fire where she literally swooned in Sheldon's arms. Somehow she found a remnant of strength to pull away. Her head dropped to his shoulder as she inhaled to clear her head and slow down her heartbeat.

"Sheldon." She'd whispered his name.

"Yes?" he gasped as he buried his face in her fragrant hair.

"Please, Sheldon," Renee pleaded, "let me go."

Slowly, deliberately he did let her go. Sheldon stared over Renee's head, his gaze meeting and fusing with Ryan's.

A smile inched up the corners of the veterinarian's mouth as he winked at his father. "We did it, Pop."

Sheldon set Renee on her feet and nodded. "Yes, *you* did."

Jeremy leaned over and pounded Sheldon's back. "We've just broken the track record!"

The words were barely out of his mouth when the employees of Blackstone Farms pumped their fists, shouting, "Boo-yaw!" The grandstand reverberated with their victory cry.

The chanting continued as Sheldon leaned over and handed Ryan two betting slips. "Take care of these after you and Jeremy stand in for me in the winner's circle." Kevin had left the box, heading for the winner's circle.

Ryan shook his head. "We can't, Pop. We're not the owners."

"Today you are," Sheldon countered. "You and Jeremy better go join Kevin and Cheryl."

Jeremy stared at his father. "You're kidding, aren't you?" He had expected Sheldon to leave the box and pose for photographers and talk to reporters from major cable sports channels, magazines and newspapers.

Sheldon shook his head. "No, I'm not."

"You can't, Pop!"

His eyes darkened like angry thunderclouds. "Please don't tell me what I can or cannot do." His expression changed like quicksilver, softening as he lowered his chin, smiled at Renee and reached for her hand. "Renee and I will meet you back at the farm."

Those in the Blackstone box stood numbly, watching as Sheldon led Renee away.

Jeremy stared at Ryan. "What's up with them?"

Ryan shook his head at the same time as he shrugged a broad shoulder under his suit jacket. "Beats the hell out of me, little brother."

Kelly looped her arm through Ryan's. "Stay out of it, darling."

He gave her a questioning stare. "Do you know something I don't?"

Kelly pressed a kiss to his smooth cheek. "I'm pleading the Fifth." She had noticed Sheldon staring at Renee, a look she was more than familiar with whenever Ryan looked at her.

Ryan opened his mouth again, but she placed her fingertips over his lips. "They are expecting the

Blackstones to join their winning horse and jockey in the winner's circle."

Ryan grasped his wife's hand and followed Jeremy and Tricia out of the box. He shook his head, grinning broadly. "Pop and a woman," he whispered to Kelly. "I suppose there is hope for the old man after all."

Sheldon helped Renee into his car before rounding the sedan to sit behind the wheel. His decision not to talk to the media was based upon his initial opposition to enter Shah Jahan in the International Gold Cup race. He'd felt the thoroughbred wasn't ready to compete, but Ryan and Jeremy had overruled him and therefore the victory was theirs.

He started up the car and left the parking area, heading for the interstate. Once he set the cruise control button, he chanced a quick glance at Renee. She sat motionless, eyes closed and her chest rising and falling gently in an even rhythm. He returned his gaze to the road in front of him before risking another glance at her flawless face. Being pregnant agreed with her. She was exquisite, her skin glowing like brown satin.

He recalled the violent expletives he'd spewed after Jeremy suggested Renee live with him until her bungalow was ready. He guarded his privacy with the zealousness of a leopard secreting his kill from marauding scavengers. He did not want someone to monitor his comings and goings. Ryan had become accustomed to his declaration of "I'm going to be away for a few days." He had made it a practice of spending two or three days each week at his mountain retreat, but that would change because of the petite woman sitting beside him.

A smile stole its way across his face as he recalled the taste and softness of her mouth and soft fullness of her breasts when he kissed her. The action had begun impulsively before it changed into a deliberate, purposeful need to possess her mouth and more. The *more* wasn't sleeping with her—that he could do with other women, but an inclination to take care of her.

Why Renee, he did not know. But in the coming months he was certain he would find out.

A slight smile played at the corners of Renee's mouth as she turned her head slightly and stared from under lowered lids at the man sitting beside her. He had discarded his suit jacket and tie, and unbuttoned the collar to his crisp white shirt. He was so virile and masculine that she forced herself to glance away.

The memory of his kiss still lingered along the fringes of her mind. The initial joining of their mouths was shocking, unexpected. But everything had changed once she kissed him back with a hunger that had belied her outward calm. The caress of his lips and the solid crush of his body had sent spirals of desire through Renee that she hadn't wanted to acknowledge, because Sheldon was her boss—a man who wore his masculinity like a badge of honor.

"Where are we going?" she asked after seeing a road sign indicating the number of miles to Staunton. The farm was in the opposite direction.

"Somewhere to celebrate." Sheldon winked at Renee when she gave him a questioning look. "Do you like ice cream?"

"Does Don King need a hair transplant?"

There was a moment of silence before deep, rumbling laughter filled the sedan. Those who were familiar with Sheldon Blackstone would have been stunned by the sound, because it had been nearly twenty years since they'd heard his unrestrained laughter. He hadn't laughed out loud since he'd become a widower.

Renee found Sheldon's laughter infectious. She joined him, and within seconds they were laughing so hard he was forced to pull over onto the shoulder of the road.

Sheldon was still smiling as he rested an arm over the back of the passenger seat. Sobering, he gave Renee a long, penetrating look and marveled that she could laugh given her circumstances. She'd walked away from a position, one in which she'd been paid well, to work on a farm because a man she'd lived with had betrayed her.

Life had dealt her two losing hands when it came to men; first her father, then her lover. Had Renee been unlucky in love or had she unconsciously fallen in love with a lover with the same failings as her father?

In another five months she would deliver a baby and he wondered whether Renee would change her mind and contact her ex to inform him that he had become a father?

The questions bombarded Sheldon as his expression changed, growing tight with a realization he did not want to think about. There was something about Renee Wilson that reminded him of his late wife, something that evoked emotions he hadn't felt since he was seventeen.

An hour after he'd been introduced to Julia he'd known he wanted to marry her. But he didn't want to marry again. The truth was he wouldn't risk his heart again to the devastation he'd felt when Julia had died. He had failed Julia as a husband and he'd long ago vowed that he would never make that mistake again. He could not propose marriage to Renee as he had with Julia, but he intended to offer her and her child his protection as long as she was a resident of Blackstone Farms. He would do no less for any employee.

He removed his arm from her seat, put the car in gear and headed for downtown Staunton.

Sheldon escorted Renee into Shorty's Diner. The popular restaurant on Richmond Road had become a favorite with locals and tourists. All stainless steel with neon lights and colorful glass, it was an exact replica of a 1950s jukebox. They were seated at the last remaining table and given menus.

Sheldon watched Renee as she looked around. "It's not fancy, but the food is good."

"Fancy doesn't always mean good," she countered. "I once ate at a Miami Beach restaurant, which will remain nameless, whose construction costs exceeded three million dollars. The food was horrific."

"Are they still open?"

"Unfortunately, yes. People go there because the owner paid off the food critic, and right now it's the place to go to be seen. The paparazzi hang around every night, hoping to get a glimpse of the celebrities who congregate there."

Reaching across the table, Sheldon placed a hand on Renee's, tightening his hold when she attempted to extract her fingers. "Do you miss Miami?"

She closed her eyes and shook her head. When she opened them she gave him a direct stare. "No, I don't. Once I decided to leave I knew I'd never go back."

He eased his grip, but did not release her hand. "What do you want?"

A slight frown furrowed her smooth forehead. "What do you mean?"

"What do you want for yourself? Your future?"

Renee could feel Sheldon's sharp eyes boring into her. His gaze was penetrating, but there was also something lazily seductive in the look. It had only taken twenty-four hours to feel the seductive pull of his spell. And if she hadn't needed a job or a place to live she would've driven away from Blackstone Farms and its owner minutes after coming face-to-face with him. Yet there was something in the light gray eyes that communicated that she could trust him to protect her and her child.

"I want to complete my probationary period without mishap, move into my own bungalow, go to law school and give birth to a healthy son or daughter. Not necessarily in that order," she added with an enchanting, dimpled smile.

A network of attractive lines fanned out around Sheldon's luminous eyes. "I certainly can help you with your probationary status. I'll tell Jeremy to waive your probationary clause."

"You can do that?"

Sheldon removed his hand. His strong jaw tensed. "I can. Besides, you don't need any added stress in your life at this time."

Renee was hard-pressed not to kiss him. A warm glow flowed through her as her features became more animated. "Thank you, Sheldon."

He angled his head and gave her a sensual smile. "You're welcome, Renee." There was a pulse beat of silence before he asked, "Are you hungry?"

She shook her head. "No. I can wait for dinner."

He closed the plastic-covered binder. "Then we'll have some ice cream."

Renee and Sheldon returned to Blackstone Farms to find Ryan sitting on the porch waiting for them. He'd changed out of his suit and into a pair of jeans, boots and a cotton V-neck sweater. He rose to his feet, his expression grim. He handed Sheldon a large manila envelope.

"I thought you should see this before it's aired later on tonight on ESPN. There's no doubt it will also appear in the *Virginian-Pilot.*"

Renee turned to make her way into the house, but Ryan reached out and touched her arm. "You should also see this, Renee."

She hadn't realized her heart was pumping wildly until she saw the photograph of her and Sheldon locked in a passionate embrace in the box at Great Meadow. The picture was taken at the exact moment she'd put her arms around his neck. The kiss had only lasted seconds, but the image of her kissing the owner of Blackstone Farms would last forever.

"Who gave this to you?" Sheldon had spoken to his son, while his gaze was fixed on Renee's shocked expression.

"Eddie Ray."

Sheldon shifted his attention on Ryan. "Are you certain it's going to be televised?"

Ryan nodded. "Eddie freelances for several tabloids and he loves uncovering scandals."

"There is no scandal," Sheldon retorted. The scowl marring his handsome face vanished as he stared at Renee. "I'm sorry to have put you in a compromising position."

Renee's smile belied her uneasiness. "Don't beat up on yourself. Neither of us can undo what has already been done."

She peered closely at the photograph. Only her profile was discernible, but the diamond studs Donald had given her as a graduation gift glittered in her lobes. Biting down on her lower lip, she prayed no one would recognize her in the arms of the man who owned Virginia's most celebrated African-American horse farm—especially Donald Rush.

She had left Florida believing Donald would never follow her; but what if he linked her to Sheldon Blackstone of Blackstone Farms and uncovered that the child she carried was his? Despite his deception, would he be vindictive enough to wage a legal battle for custody? There was no way she could win against a man who had amassed millions of dollars as a toy manufacturer. Unshed tears glistened in her eyes.

"I have to go inside." She had to get away from Ryan and Sheldon before she embarrassed herself.

Sheldon watched the screen door open and close behind Renee's departing figure. He waited a full minute, then let loose with a diatribe that included what he wanted to do to Eddie Ray.

Ryan slipped his hands into the pockets of his jeans, rocking back on his heels. "Folks outside the farm are going to want to know who the mystery woman is."

"Who she is is none of their damn business!"

"There's already been talk, Pop."

"What about?" Sheldon snapped angrily.

"About you and Renee. You were all over her last night like white on rice, and today at the track the two of you looked like a..." His words trailed off.

"We looked like what?"

Ryan ignored his father's angry glare. "A couple."

"Is that how you see us, Ryan? As a couple?"

The veterinarian gave a sheepish grin. "From what I've seen of the two of you—yes."

Sheldon put the photograph into the envelope and thrust it at Ryan. "Go home to your wife and children," he drawled. Turning, he pushed open the screen door and walked into his house.

He had to talk to Renee and reassure her that he would do everything in his power to protect her from salacious gossip. Horse farms had all of the characteristics of a small town. Any rumor was a prerequisite for scandal. Climbing the staircase to the second floor, he made his way along the hallway. Her bedroom door stood open. He rapped lightly. There was no response; he knocked again, then walked in.

Renee sat on a chair in the sitting room, her bare feet resting on a matching footstool. Although her eyes were closed, he knew she was not asleep.

"Renee?"

Her eyes opened and she stared at him as if he were a stranger. Her lower lip trembled as she smiled through the moisture shimmering in her gold-brown eyes. "I'm okay," she lied smoothly.

The truth was she wasn't okay, because if Donald saw the photograph he would know the identity of the woman in Sheldon Blackstone's arms.

Sheldon did not believe Renee. She looked delicate, vulnerable. He moved closer, reached down and pulled her gently off the chair. He gathered her to his chest, resting his chin on the top of her head.

"What are you afraid of, Renee?"

She tried to slow down her runaway heartbeat. "What makes you think I'm afraid?"

"You're trembling."

The possibility that Donald would attempt to contact her at Blackstone Farms held her captive with fear. "I don't want him to find me," she sobbed against Sheldon's chest.

Cradling her face between his palms, he kissed her eyelids, his tongue capturing the moisture streaking her cheeks. "Don't cry, baby." She quieted as he comforted her, his hand moving over her spine. "Who is he, princess?"

She sighed softly. "His name is Donald Rush."

"What does he do?"

"He's a successful toy manufacturer."

Easing back, Sheldon anchored a hand under her chin and raised her tear-stained face. "You will be safe here. No one, and I mean no one, can come onto the property without being detected. And if he comes after you, then we'll have a surprise for him."

"What?"

"He'll be shot for trespassing."

Renee smiled despite her anxiety. "I hope it won't come to that."

"The decision will be his. Enough about Donald Rush." A frown settled into his features. "Now, we have to talk about you and me."

Her eyes widened. "What about us?"

"Ryan reports there's been gossip about us being a couple."

Her mouth dropped open. "But we're not," she said, recovering her voice.

"*We* know that. But, what's going to happen once your condition becomes evident?"

Pulling out of Sheldon's loose embrace, Renee walked over to a window and stared down at the leaves of a towering tree that had turned a brilliant red-orange. She turned and met his gaze.

"You think they'll believe I'm carrying your baby?"

Sheldon closed the distance between them. "I'm certain some people will believe that."

"What are we going to do, Sheldon?"

He crossed his arms over his chest. "Let them believe whatever they want."

She raised her eyebrows. "You don't care?"

"No. I stopped listening to gossip a long time ago."

"What do you propose?" Renee asked.

"Let me take care of you," Sheldon said without hesitating.

Renee's mind was spinning in bewilderment. Why was Sheldon giving her double messages? He'd said they weren't a couple—and they weren't. Then in the next breath he'd offered to take care of her.

"How?"

"Live here with me until the spring and become my hostess at all social events on and off the farm."

Her eyelids fluttered, her emotions spun out of control and she tried to digest his proposition. Not only would she work for Sheldon, but she would also live with him beyond the time he had projected her bungalow would be ready for occupancy. She would also become an actress whenever she stepped into a role as his date at social functions.

"Will this arrangement be on a strictly business level?"

Sheldon studied Renee thoughtfully for a moment. His eyes drank in her delicate face, unaware of the smoldering invitation in their silvery depths.

"It would be if I were your boss," he said in a deep, quiet voice.

She blinked once. "But you are my boss."

"Effective midnight, October thirty-first, I will officially retire as CEO of Blackstone Farms."

"But that's next week." There was no mistaking the shock in her voice.

Sheldon nodded. "I can't ask you to host a party for me if I'm your boss. That would be slimy *and* unethical."

Let me take care of you. His words came rushing back, and Renee stared at the man who within twenty-four hours had offered her what neither her father nor Donald had or could: his protection.

Tilting her chin in a defiant gesture, Renee gave him a challenging look. "You didn't answer my question, Mr. Sheldon Blackstone. Business or pleasure?"

He leaned in close, close enough for his breath to caress her cheek. "That decision will have to be yours, Miss Renee Wilson."

Renee felt in control for the first time since viewing the photograph. Sheldon was so compelling that her heart fluttered wildly in her breast. His nearness was overwhelming, presence potent.

Smiling, she said softly, "Strictly business."

Sheldon nodded, dipped his head and brushed his mouth over hers. He pulled back. "Business it is."

Renee stood, rooted to the spot as Sheldon turned and walked out of her bedroom. Once she realized what she'd agreed to, she floated down to the armchair and rested her bare feet on the tapestry footstool.

Living at Blackstone Farms would give her a

chance to heal as she prepared for a new life for herself and her unborn child. However, she had to be very careful, because she had no intention of permitting herself to succumb to Sheldon Blackstone's intoxicatingly sensual spell.

Four

The televised footage of the International Gold Cup and the image of her kissing Sheldon were both aired on ESPN, compounding her anxiety that Donald might recognize her.

Renee existed in a state of fear, believing that Donald would show up at Blackstone Farms demanding to see her. One day became two and eventually a week before she was finally able to relax.

She found the cooler morning and evening temperatures a welcome respite from Miami's sultry heat and humidity, and the task of bringing Blackstone Farms into the electronic age challenging. It had taken a day to set up a system for an electronic payroll procedure and two more to program a database for purchase orders. Her respect for Sheldon increased appreciably once she realized the amount of money needed for a horse farm's viability. And despite the glitter and glamour of pre- and post-race parties the behind-the-scenes work was ongoing: feeding, grooming and exercising thirty-four thoroughbreds, mucking out stalls, daily medical checkups for lameness and other equine maladies and the repair of paddocks and posts.

A knock on her office door garnered her attention. Swiveling on her chair, she saw Sheldon's broad shoulders filling out the doorway. Dressed in a pair of jeans, boots and pullover sweater, he presented a formidable figure in black.

She gave him a bright smile. "Good afternoon."

Sheldon winked at her. "Good afternoon. I came to tell you that Kelly has recruited us to help make jack-o'-lanterns."

It was Friday, Halloween and an official Blackstone Farms school holiday. The faculty and staff had organized a read-a-thon for students, in grades four to six, reading from the works of Mary Wollstonecraft Shelley, Bram Stoker, Edgar Allan Poe and J.K. Rowling.

Renee raised her eyebrows. "I've never made a jack-o'-lantern."

Sheldon studied Renee. He'd found her fresh-scrubbed face and her hair piled haphazardly atop her head innocently alluring. The image of her in his bed and her hair spread over his pillow popped into his head and popped out just as quickly. He did not want to lump her into the category of the other women who'd shared his bed, but would never share his life.

He had deliberately avoided her because he needed to know whether he was attracted to her because of her feminine sensuality or because he really liked Renee Wilson.

Even though he had kept his distance, he still could not stop thinking about her. It was October thirty-first, the day he intended to announce his retirement. After today, he intended to openly pursue her, hopefully satisfying his curiosity.

"It gets easier after you mutilate your first dozen or so."

The dimples in her cheeks deepened as her smile widened. "What happens to the ones that don't make it?"

"They become pies."

She wrinkled her nose. "How very convenient. Give me a minute to save these files."

Sheldon watched Renee shut down her computer and put her desk in order. If he had had any doubts as to her qualifications they were quickly dashed once she convinced Jeremy to set up the farm's payroll account with a local bank that offered service-free accounts to new depositors. Actual payroll checks would be replaced with electronic transfers, thereby eliminating the need for paper.

Renee turned off the desk lamp and stood up. "Where are we going to create these masterpieces?"

"The school's cafeteria." Sheldon glanced down at her feet. She had on a pair of sensible low-heeled boots. "Do you feel up to walking?" The school was a quarter of a mile from his house.

"I don't mind walking, but I will need a jacket." The oversized cotton knit tunic was perfect for moderate afternoon temperatures, but Renee doubted whether it would be adequate after the sun set.

Extending his hand, Sheldon closed the distance between them. "If it gets too cool for you I'll get someone to drive you back."

"What about you?"

"The cool weather doesn't bother me."

Renee placed her hand in Sheldon's, smiling when he squeezed her fingers gently. There were calluses on his palms, indicating he was certainly no stranger to hard work.

Waiting until they had stepped out into the bright early afternoon sunlight, Renee asked, "How did you get into the horse-racing business?"

A faraway look filled his eyes as he pondered the question, contemplating how much he wanted to tell Renee about his past. He decided to be forthcoming.

"I hadn't planned on racing horses. My father was a tobacco farmer, as was his father before him. They grew and harvested some of the finest tobacco in the state, but that ended when my mother died from lung cancer. She had a two-pack-a-day cigarette habit that literally consumed her. As she lay dying she made Dad promise two things: marry her and stop growing tobacco."

"Did he marry her?"

Sheldon nodded. "Yes, but it was not what you would consider a legal union."

Renee glanced up at his distinctive profile. "Why not?"

A muscle in his jaw tensed. "My mother worked for him."

A tense silence enveloped them as they walked. "Your father was white and your mother black," Renee stated after a prolonged silence. Sheldon's eye color, hair texture and features were characteristic of someone of mixed blood.

The tense lines in his face relaxed, and Sheldon nodded again. "Virginia's miscegenation law would not permit them to marry."

"But you say they were married."

"There was no license nor any record of the marriage at the courthouse. A black minister who swore an oath of secrecy performed the ceremony. James Blackstone buried his wife, and three months later harvested his last tobacco crop.

"Dad took his life savings and bought twenty-two horses. It's ironic that he knew nothing about breeding horses, but told everyone he was a quick learner. And he was right. He made huge profits selling horses to farmers and for riding.

"He wanted me to go to college, then eventually take over from him. But I told him I didn't want to be a horse breeder. We argued constantly. After one particularly hostile exchange, I drove to Richmond and enlisted in the army."

"How old were you?"

"Seventeen. I know it broke Dad's heart because he knew I would be sent to Vietnam. I went to South Carolina for basic training, met a girl there, fell in love and married her before I was shipped out. I was assigned to Special Forces and trained as a sniper."

Renee remembered his comment about shooting trespassers. "Did you and your father ever reconcile?"

"Yes. After Julia wrote and told me she was pregnant, she went to live with Dad."

"Why didn't she stay with her folks?"

"They felt she had disgraced them by marrying out of her social circle."

Renee's delicate jaw dropped. "You're joking?"

"I wish," Sheldon drawled. "Julia's family, the Grants, believe they are the black elite, aristocrats of color."

Sheldon released Renee's hand, curved an arm around her waist, picked her up and moved quickly off the road. Within seconds a pickup truck sped past them.

She leaned into Sheldon; her heart pounded in her

chest as he set her on her feet. She hadn't heard the truck. "You must have ears like a bat."

He smiled down at her. "If you live here long enough you'll be able to hear a frog croak a mile away."

Tilting her chin, Renee met his amused gaze. "I like living here. I thought it would be boring and much too quiet after living in Miami."

"I'm glad you like living here, because I like you, Renee."

"Thank you. It makes it easier to work together if we like each other."

His light gray eyes captured her warm gold-brown ones. "I don't think you understand my liking."

"What is there to understand, Sheldon?" she argued softly. "You *like* me."

Tightening his hold on her waist, he pulled her gently under a copse of trees. "I don't think you understand how much I like you, Renee. Maybe I should show you." Lowering his head slowly, deliberately, he brushed his lips against hers.

Renee clung to him like a drowning swimmer as his warm, moist, demanding mouth called, and she answered the call. This kiss was nothing like the one they'd shared in the box at Great Meadow. It was persuasive, coaxing. A fire she had not felt in a long time flared to life, and standing on tiptoe she opened her mouth to his probing tongue. Curving her arms under his shoulders, she communicated silently that she liked him, too—a lot.

She had spent a week telling herself that she had not been affected by Sheldon's kiss, that she did not find him attractive and that their agreement to pose as a couple was preposterous.

She had told herself that women gave birth to babies every day without a husband or a man in their lives, yet with each month bringing her closer to motherhood she knew that was not the kind of life she wanted for herself. She wanted someone with her whenever she went for her checkups; someone to massage her aching back and legs because she wasn't used to carrying the extra weight; someone with her in the delivery room to share her joy once she brought her son or daughter into the world.

She wanted that and so much more, but refused to think of the more.

Sheldon couldn't get enough of Renee. He kissed her mouth, the end of her nose, her eyes and then moved to the hollow of her fragrant throat. Nothing mattered except the woman in his arms.

He smiled when Renee giggled softly. "What are you laughing at?" he whispered in her ear.

"You," she whispered back. "I think you've made your point."

As he eased back, his gaze caught and held hers. "I don't think I have."

Her smile faded, and the pulse in her throat fluttered erratically, making swallowing difficult. "What are you talking about?"

Sheldon pressed a kiss to her ear. "I'm a little rusty when it comes to the dating game, so you're going to have to help me out before we make our debut as a couple."

Renee anchored her palms against his chest, pushing him back. "When?"

"Next month. I've committed to attend the wedding of a friend's daughter."

She rested her hands on her hips. "Next month," she repeated. "Tomorrow is next month."

"It's three weeks from now."

"Three weeks will give me enough time to shop for something to wear. My body is changing rapidly." He reached for her, but she moved out of arm's reach. "If you need me to act as your date or hostess you're going to have to let me know well in advance, because I'm extremely busy. After all, I do work nine-to-five, and I also have to have time to see my obstetrician."

The mention of an obstetrician sobered Sheldon as if he had been doused with cold water. Although Renee's body hadn't displayed the obvious signs of her pregnancy he was always cognizant that she was carrying another man's child—a man from whom she was hiding.

He nodded. "I'll give you the dates and events of my social commitments. I'll also take you to Staunton tomorrow so you can shop for whatever you need. Does this meet with your approval, princess?" he teased.

She affected an attractive moue, curtseying gracefully. "Yes, your highness."

Laughing, Sheldon reached for her hand and they returned to the road. "Look," he said, pointing upward.

Renee squinted up at a large bird flying in a circle. "Is that a hawk?"

"Yes. There was a time when we didn't see too many of them. But since it's illegal to kill them they've made a comeback."

Sheldon waved to two men in a truck going in the opposite direction, the cab of the pickup loaded with fencing to replace the worn posts along the undeveloped north section of the property, property he had deeded to his grandchildren.

He had purchased the two thousand additional acres because of rumors that a developer wanted to erect half a dozen subdivisions on the site. New homes meant an influx of people, cars and pollution that would impact on the natural beauty of the horse farms with stately manor homes, miles of forests divided by hedges, white rail fences and stone walls. He had joined the other farm owners whose mission was to halt the encroachment of development in the region.

Renee walked into Blackstone Day School's cafeteria to a flurry of activity as a group of women carved faces into pumpkins, while Kelly and Tricia Blackstone filled cartons with already carved specimens wearing funny and grotesque cutout expressions.

The school that had begun as an early childhood care center was expanded to include up to grade six. The children from Blackstone Farms and many others from neighboring farms had become recipients of a superior education taught by a staff of highly qualified teachers.

Kelly glanced up, flashing a smile when she spied her father-in-law and Renee. "Thank you guys for coming."

"How many do you have left?" Sheldon asked.

"About sixty."

Renee stared at the small round pumpkins lining the stainless steel countertop. Their stems, tops and seeds had been removed. "How many have you carved?"

Kelly wiped the back of her hand over her forehead. "I lost count after a hundred and thirty."

Sitting on a stool, Renee picked up a small knife with a wicked-looking curved blade. She stared at Ryan's wife. It was the first time she noticed the absence of a southern drawl in her beautifully modulated voice.

"Why do you carve so many?"

"You'll see why after they're lighted," Kelly said mysteriously.

Renee's curiosity was piqued. "Do you light them with candles?"

Kelly nodded. "Tea lights."

Sheldon sat down next to Renee and picked up a marker. "How artistic are you?"

She wrinkled her nose. "Not very," she admitted.

He handed her the marker. "Draw your face, then I'll show you how to use the knife."

Renee drew two hearts for the eyes, a circle for a nose and a crooked grin for the mouth. She gave Sheldon her pumpkin and within seconds he'd cut out a face sporting a silly-looking expression.

"Very, very nice, princess," he crooned.

"Thank you," she whispered back.

They spent the next two hours making jack-o'-lanterns. This year's jack-o'-lantern production differed from the prior ones. Only ten pumpkins would be turned into pies.

Renee sat at a table in the dining hall with Sheldon, Jeremy and Tricia, totally amused by the number of children outfitted as hunchbacks, werewolves, pirates, skeletons, vampires, princesses, clowns and a popular wrestler. It was the first time school-age children and their parents from the other horse farms had come for the Halloween holiday celebration.

The dining room staff had prepared a buffet feast reflecting the holiday: dem rattlin' bones spareribs; tombstone taters: baked potatoes with bacon, grated cheddar cheese and sour cream; creepy crawlers: shrimp served with a Cajun sauce in a spicy mayonnaise; deviled eggs; devil's food cake and peanut butter cupcakes. A large bowl was filled warm nonalcoholic apple cider.

Sheldon stood up, waiting until the babble of

voices became a hush, followed by complete silence. His silvery gaze swept over those whom he had come to regard as his extended family. They were hard-working, loyal people who were directly responsible for the farm's success.

A melancholy expression flitted across his features. "I'd like to welcome our neighbors to Blackstone Farms' annual Halloween celebration, hoping you'll enjoy yourself enough to come again next year. I say this because I will not stand here next year to meet and greet you because I'm retiring—tonight." His announcement was followed by gasps.

Ryan leaned back in his chair at a nearby table and stared at Jeremy; their expressions mirrored confusion. Sheldon nodded to Jeremy before repeating the gesture with Ryan.

Sheldon knew he'd shocked his sons with the announcement that he was stepping down two months early. He'd decided not to tell Ryan and Jeremy because he was certain there would be a confrontation. He'd spent the past year dropping hints that he wanted to retire because he'd tired of the day-to-day responsibility of running the farm, while they'd spent the past year denying the inevitable.

"I've waited thirty years for this day, and I'm blessed to have two sons who will accomplish feats I can only dream about. Jeremy, Ryan, I love and trust you to continue Blackstone Farms' quest for the Triple Crown."

Kevin pumped his fist, shouting, "Boo-yaw! Boo-yaw! *Boo-yaw!*"

The Blackstone victory cry reverberated throughout the dining hall as others joined in. Sheldon held up a hand until the room grew quiet again.

"Ryan and Jeremy will share equal control of the farm. Jeremy will be responsible for finance and personnel, and Ryan will provide day-to-day oversight." He had selected Jeremy as the chief fiscal officer because he'd earned a business degree from Stanford. Turning to Jeremy, he extended his hand. "Now, please get up and say something profound."

Renee watched Jeremy lean over and kiss his wife before coming to his feet. He'd brushed his rakishly long black hair off his face, revealing tiny diamond studs in his pierced lobes. There was no doubt the next generation of Blackstones would march to the beat of their own drum.

Jeremy flashed a crooked smile as everyone applauded. He gave Sheldon a quick glance. "My father asked that I say something profound. To tell you the truth I really can't come up with anything except to say that hopefully twenty years from now I can stand here and pass the torch to my nephew Sean."

Five-year-old Sean waved his fist the way he'd seen his father, grandfather and uncle do. "Boo-yaw, Uncle Jeremy." The room erupted in laughter.

Placing two fingers to his forehead, Jeremy saluted Sean. "Boo-yaw to you, too, champ. I know everyone wants to eat and celebrate the holiday, so I leave you with this. Shah Jahan and Cheryl will accomplish what no other horse has done in decades. They *will* win the Triple Crown." The Boo-yaws started up again as people came over to the table to wish Jeremy the best.

Looping her arm through Sheldon's, Renee asked, "Who or what is Boo-yaw?"

Sheldon covered the small hand on his arm. "He was our first champion." He had been their first Derby winner and the last race Julia attended. A week later she'd died in his arms.

He smiled down at her. "After we eat we'll take a hayride."

She glanced up at him from under a fringe of thick lashes. "I hope you don't think I'm going to roll around in the hay with you."

Throwing back his head, Sheldon let loose with a peal of laughter. The room went suddenly quiet as everyone turned and stared at him. He sobered quickly, returned their stares until their attention was refocused elsewhere. Renee tried to suppress a giggle, but she was unsuccessful. Burying her face against Sheldon's shoulder, she laughed until her sides hurt.

Curving a hand around her neck, Sheldon whispered, "I'm going to get you for that, Renee."

"I'm so-o-o-o scared, Sheldon," she said, still laughing.

"You should be," he countered. His hand trailed down her spine, coming to rest on a rounded hip. She went completely still as her gaze widened. "Now, say something else," he threatened softly.

The warmth of his hand penetrated the fabric of her slacks, and Renee was hard-pressed not to squirm in her chair. She met his gaze as he looked at her as if he were photographing her with his eyes. He had stoked a gently growing fire she was powerless to control.

She had left Florida because of one man, and had come to Virginia to start over. It had only taken a week and she found herself falling under the spell of another man who made her want him in spite of herself.

The very air around them seemed electrified with a waiting, a waiting for the next move. Sheldon's nearness made her senses spin as his potent energy wrapped around her in a sensual cocoon that made her want to take off her clothes and lie with him.

A hint of a smile softened her mouth as she fluttered her lashes. "Please get me something to eat before I faint on you."

Sheldon removed his hand, stood up and pushed back his chair in one motion. She watched him as he cut the line. Three minutes later he returned to the table and set a plate on the table in front of her. "What do you want to drink, princess?"

"Milk. Please make certain it's fat-free and ice-cold."

Sheldon flashed a saccharine grin, then left to do her bidding. He didn't know whether he was good for Renee, but knew for certain she was good for him.

She made him laugh, something he hadn't done in years. And she made him look forward to his retirement with the expectation of a young child opening gifts on Christmas Day.

Yes, he thought, he was going to enjoy being a couple.

Five

Hundreds of lighted jack-o'-lanterns lined the roads of Blackstone Farms like an airport runway; a full moon, the second in the month, silvered the countryside in an eerie glow added to the magic of the night.

The cool night air seeped through the fibers of Renee's bulky pullover sweater, and she snuggled closer to Sheldon, sharing his body's heat. She had taken her first hayride in a horse-drawn wagon. The driver stopped, dropping off and picking up passengers along a northbound route; children gathered on padded mats in the schoolyard, crowded around a large oil drum from which blazed a bonfire, listening to ghost stories while eating cotton candy, popcorn and candied apples.

She sat on the grass with Sheldon and stared up at the star-littered sky. "The moon looks close enough to touch." Her soft voice whispered over Sheldon's throat.

Sheldon pressed his mouth to her hair. "The second full moon in any month is called a blue moon. However, Native Americans have named every full moon in the calendar."

"What are the names?"

"January is full wolf moon, February full snow moon and March full worm moon."

"What do they call October?"

"Full hunter's moon."

"How do you know so much about Native American folklore?"

"Growing up my best friend was a Delaware Nanticoke boy. His family moved to Virginia the year he turned four."

"Where is he now?"

There was a moment of silence before Sheldon said, "He died in Vietnam."

Shifting, Renee put an arm around his neck and rested her head on his shoulder. She was sorry she'd asked because each time she questioned Sheldon about someone the subject of death surfaced: his mother, his wife and now a childhood friend. His life was filled with the loss of loved ones while hers had been filled with disappointment.

"I'm sorry." The two words, though whispered, sounded unusually loud.

"I'm not sorry you're here," Sheldon mumbled in her hair.

A smile lifted her mouth. "Why?"

"Because you make me laugh, Renee."

"Are you saying I'm funny or silly?"

A chuckle rumbled in his chest. "No. It's just that you're good for me. You remind me that life shouldn't be so serious."

"I'm glad I can make you laugh."

Sheldon tightened his hold around her waist. "What do you want from me?"

Renee refused to acknowledge the significance of his query. Did he actually want her to tell him what she wanted from him as a man? That she wanted to trust a man enough to protect her and her child?

Could she tell Sheldon that the more time she spent with him the more confused she became? That her feelings for him intensified each time he touched or kissed her.

"I want a friend," she said instead. "Someone I can confide in, someone who will laugh and cry with me in the good and not so good…." Her words trailed off as she realized how vulnerable and needy she must sound to Sheldon.

His warm breath caressed her parted lips as he lowered his head and tasted her mouth.

"What do you want from me, Sheldon?" Her query was a shivery whisper.

Sheldon pulled her closer. "I want to be your best

friend, I want to protect you *and* your child and I'd like you to live with me."

"But I am living with you," she countered.

"No, Renee, we are sharing a house."

Strange and disquieting thoughts swirled through Renee, his words not registering on her dizzied senses. "You want sex?"

A low, rumbling laugh bubbled from his throat. "Why do you make it sound so sordid?"

"Because I tell it like it is?"

Sheldon sobered. "You've misunderstood me, Renee. I've been widowed a long time, and until meeting you I had no idea how lonely I've been." His lips came coaxingly down on hers. "I want companionship, princess."

Parting her lips and swallowing his breath, Renee kissed Sheldon leisurely, lingering and savoring his scent, the feel of his firm mouth. There was no mistaking the hardness he pressed against her. She smothered a groan and bit down on her lower lip. The urge to roll her hips against him was so strong that it frightened her.

Her hands came up and cradled his face, thumbs sweeping over the elegant ridge of his cheekbones. He was offering her everything she wanted and needed, everything except marriage. But even without a promise of marriage she wondered whether she could trust him?

"I don't know, Sheldon." *I don't know if I can trust you,* she added silently.

He placed a forefinger over her lips. "You don't have to give me an answer. Come to me when you're ready."

"What if I'm never ready?"

"Then we'll remain best friends."

Renee lowered her hands, curving her arms under Sheldon's shoulders. They sat motionless, holding each other until the sound of the approaching wagon propelled them off the ground for the ride back to the main house.

The sound of tires crunching gravel drowned out the cacophony of nocturnal sounds serenading the countryside. A knowing smile curved Sheldon's mouth as he waited for his late-night visitors. Renee had retired to bed, but he hadn't been able to sleep. His mind was too active, too wound up after he'd bared his soul to Renee. He left bed, pulled on a sweatshirt over a pair of jeans, then came downstairs to sit on the porch.

Vulnerability, something he hadn't experienced in years, had slipped under the barrier he had erected to keep all women at a distance. The women who knew him were aware that he would offer them his passion, but never his heart. However, in the span of a single week a woman had unknowingly woven her way into his life and into his heart.

Sheldon sat forward on the rocker. The sound of doors closing was followed by booted footfalls on the porch steps. "What took you so long?"

Ryan climbed the stairs and sat on the glider, leaving his brother to take the chaise. "You were expecting us?"

Sheldon gave Ryan a long, penetrating stare. "But of course."

"Are you all right, Pop?"

Sheldon shifted his attention to Jeremy. "I'm fine," he countered sharply. "Why would you me ask that?"

Jeremy ignored his father's clipped tone. "You announced your retirement without giving us prior warning."

"I told you I was retiring at the end of the year. But with Jahan's win I decided to push it up."

Clasping his hands between his knees, Ryan leaned forward. "Are you sure that's the reason, Pop?"

Sheldon's jaw tightened as he glared at Ryan before pinning his angry gaze on Jeremy. "What's going on here?"

"Jeremy and I…we thought that something might be wrong and you were trying to conceal it from us."

Realization slowly dawned. Sheldon closed his eyes and shook his head. This scene was a repeat of one that had occurred twenty-one years before. He'd sat down with his sons and told them their mother was ill—terminally ill. Julia had discovered a lump in her breast, but refused to go to a doctor until it was too late. She'd waited until after Boo-yaw's Derby victory to tell her husband that she was dying. Her excuse was that she hadn't wanted to bother him.

It had been the first and only time he'd raised his voice to his wife. His tirade ended with him weeping in her arms because he hadn't been there for Julia when she needed him. That had been the first and last time he'd let anyone see him cry.

Sheldon opened his eyes. "There's nothing wrong with me."

Jeremy's dove-gray eyes narrowed. "Are you sure, Pop?"

"Do you want to see the results of my latest physical?"

"No, Pop." Jeremy reached over and patted Sheldon's shoulder. "I'm just glad you're okay."

"Me, too," said Ryan. "Sometimes it's hard to tell with you because your moods run hot and cold."

Jeremy winked at Sheldon. "I've noticed lately that you're running more hot than cold. Does a Miss Wilson have anything to do with that?"

There was a long pause before Sheldon said, "Yes."

Ryan moved off the glider and thumped his father's solid back. "Good for you."

"Boo-yaw!" Jeremy said in a loud whisper.

A flash of humor crossed Sheldon's face before his expression changed, becoming somber. "Thank you for worrying about your old man."

Jeremy swung denim-covered legs over the side of the chaise and stood up. "You're not old, Pop. We just don't want anything to happen to you. Tricia and I would like to give you at least three grandchildren before we turn forty."

Sheldon nodded his approval. "What about you, Ryan?"

"Kelly and I talked about having one more."

Sheldon nodded again. "Six grandchildren. I like the sound of that."

"Good night, Pop," Ryan and Jeremy said in unison as they prepared to take their leave.

"Good night," Sheldon said in a quiet voice. He felt as if a weight had been lifted from his chest. He'd even surprised himself after admitting to Jeremy and Ryan that he was attracted to Renee; he'd never disclosed his involvement with a woman to them before. He suspected his sons believed he had been celibate for the past two decades. That meant for twenty-one years he had successfully kept his private life private. All of that would change in a month once he attended the wedding with Renee, he thought with a wry smile.

Sheldon and Renee left the farm Saturday morning for Staunton. On the way they shared a gourmet brunch at the Frederick House, a small hotel with a tearoom in the European tradition.

Sheldon left her at a specialty boutique, promising to return in an hour. The one hour became two as she tried on undergarments, tunics, slacks and dresses that artfully camouflaged her fuller breasts and expanding waistline.

She finally emerged from the dressing room to find Sheldon sitting on a delicate chair reading a newspaper. His head came up slowly. Smiling, he stood up.

"Are you ready?"

Her gaze met his. "I have to pay for my purchases."

He took her arm. "I already paid for them. They'll be delivered to the farm Monday."

Renee tried escaping his firm grip, but his fingers tightened like manacles. "I don't need you to pay for my clothes."

"Let's not argue *here,*" he warned in a dangerously soft tone.

"No. Let's not," she retorted between her teeth. Seething, she followed him through the rear of the boutique and into the adjacent parking lot. "I don't need or want you to pay for anything for me."

Sheldon opened the passenger side door to his pickup truck, caught her around the waist and swung her up to the seat. He glared at her, then closed the door with a solid slam.

Once it became apparent that he wasn't going to respond to her protests, Renee crossed her arms under her breasts and stared out the windshield. Sheldon took his seat beside her, turned on the engine and shifted into gear. The silence inside the vehicle swelled to a deafening pitch.

She did not want Sheldon to believe she was destitute. Although she'd lived with Donald she also had retained her independence. She paid her own bills, and when Donald offered to give her one of his many cars, she had refused it. In the end she was able to walk away with what had belonged to her and her dignity.

"I have to make a stop." Sheldon's voice broke the silence five minutes later. He pulled into a parking space at a supermarket.

"I'll wait here for you," Renee mumbled.

He shrugged a shoulder. "Suit yourself." He left the truck and made his way into the store. She was still pouting when he got into the truck and handed her a large paper sack.

"You can repay me for *that* if you want to."

Renee peered into the bag. It held two half-gallon bottles of fat-free milk. "Very funny, Sheldon," she said, biting back a smile.

"Think of it as a peace offering."

"How can it be a peace offering when we haven't had a fight?"

Suddenly his face went grim. "And we won't. We may not agree on everything, but one thing I will not do is fight with you." He had made it a practice never to argue with a woman. It was not his style.

"Why did you pay for my clothes?"

"Because I asked you to go out with me, not the other way around. Does that answer your question?"

There was a pulse beat of silence before Renee nodded. "Yes, it does."

His expression softened. "Good."

Resting his right arm over the back of her seat, he trailed his fingertips over the nape of her neck. "How would you like to hang out with me for the rest of the day?"

Renee shivered as much from the feathery stroking motions on the sensitive skin as from the gray orbs boring into her with a silent expectation. It was easy, too easy, to get lost in the way he was looking at her. She studied his face, feature by feature, committing them to memory while curbing the urge to trace the shape of his black curving eyebrows, the bridge of his aquiline nose and firm mouth with her fingers.

Desire, want and need swooped at her innards, and she shuttered her gaze quickly before he read her licentious thoughts. Sheldon Blackstone was the first man she'd met who made her want him just by staring.

"Okay, Sheldon. I'll hang out with you." She heard his audible sigh. It was apparent he'd been holding his breath.

Leaning closer, he pressed a kiss to her forehead. "Thank you."

Sheldon took the sack with the milk off her lap and put in a space behind the seats, then drove out of the supermarket's parking lot, heading in a westerly direction.

* * *

Renee woke up ninety minutes later surrounded by towering pine trees. The truck had stopped. Her lids fluttered as she peered through the windshield at the forested area.

"Where are we?"

Sheldon got out and came around to assist her. "Minnehaha Springs."

Dry leaves and pine cones crackled under their booted feet. "Are we still in Virginia?"

"Yes. But we're only fifteen miles from the West Virginia state line." Wrapping an arm around her waist over a lightweight jacket, Sheldon led Renee toward a house erected in the middle of a clearing. "Let's go inside the cabin, because once the sun sets the temperature drops quickly."

Renee glanced up at a structure that looked more like a chalet than a cabin. She waited as Sheldon unlocked the front door and touched a panel on the wall. Within seconds the entire first floor was flooded with golden light. She walked in, staring at a stone fireplace spanning an entire wall.

Sheldon reached for her hand. "This is where I hang out whenever I need to get away from the farm."

Her stunned gaze swept over a space that was comparable to the health spa she had frequented in South Beach. Ceiling fans, track lighting, skylights, gleaming wood floors, white-on-white furnishings, floor-to-ceiling windows and a wrought-iron staircase leading to a second-story loft provided the backdrop for a space that invited one to enter—and stay awhile.

"It's beautiful."

"It's peaceful," Sheldon countered. "Wait here while I get the milk from the truck, then I'll give you a tour."

The house contained three bedrooms. The master bedroom and bath took up the entire loft. There were two other bedrooms on the first floor. The larger had an adjoining bath with a massive sunken tub, freestanding shower and a steam room. A full, functional kitchen, living/dining area and a family room completed a space constructed for maximum living, dining and relaxing comfort.

Renee sat in the kitchen on a tall stool, munching on raw carrots, washing them down with milk and watching Sheldon as he rubbed ground spices onto the steaks he had taken from the freezer and quickly defrosted in the microwave.

Her gaze moved leisurely over his tall, slender body. He moved around the kitchen slicing and sautéing foods as if he'd performed the tasks on a daily basis. Then she remembered his mother had been a cook.

"Are you certain you don't want me to help you?"

He gave her a sidelong glance before he focused his attention to the temperature gauge on the stovetop grill. "Don't you know how to sit and relax?"

"I sit all day."

Drying his hands on a towel, Sheldon closed the distance between them and hugged her. "After you have your baby you'll look back on this moment and wished you'd taken advantage of it."

Renee went completely still. It was the first time Sheldon had made reference to her having a baby since the day of the race. She found it odd that he was willing to be seen with her in public when there was certain to be gossip once her condition became evident.

Tilting her chin, she stared up at him staring down at her. "You're probably right."

"I know I'm right. It's not easy for a woman to balance work and motherhood. That's the reason I set up the farm's child-care center. Some of the mothers wanted to go back to school to either begin or resume careers, but couldn't find anyone to watch their children. With Tricia as the school's pediatric nurse most of them don't have to miss days if their children aren't feeling well. It will be even easier for you because you work on the farm."

"Having on-site child care was the reason I accepted the position."

Sheldon wanted to tell Renee that he was glad she had been hired. Once he'd acknowledged his growing attraction for her he thought about her unborn child, asking himself whether he wanted to become involved with a woman with a baby when his youngest son, at thirty-two, was going to make him a grandfather for the third time. He had taken early retirement at fifty-three to kick back and relax, not play surrogate father.

The questions had bombarded him when he least expected them, and the answer was always the same: yes. Yes, because Renee made him laugh—something he hadn't done in a long time. And yes, because she unknowingly had elicited from him a profound longing for a woman he hadn't felt in years. What amazed him was that she hadn't flirted with him as some women did. She had just been herself. He had found her strong, independent, but whenever the topic of her ex came up she exhibited a vulnerability that made him want to do everything in his power to protect her.

Sheldon reached up and wiped a residue of milk from her top lip with his thumb. "Did you drink a lot of milk before you got pregnant?"

Dimples winked in her flawless cheeks as she gave him a warm smile. "No. Instead of craving potato chips and pickles like other women, I have an insatiable thirst for milk."

"Milk is a lot healthier than chips and pickles." He kissed the end of her nose. "When are you scheduled to go to the doctor?"

A slight frown appeared between Renee's eyes. "Next Friday. Why?"

"I'll go with you."

She stared, complete surprise on her face, as an

unexpected warmth eddied through her. She wanted to ask Sheldon why, but the word was lodged in her constricted throat.

Renee nodded her consent, not trusting herself to speak. He was offering her what she wanted, someone to accompany her when she went for her checkups. Her sister-in-law had gone with her the first three times, and she hadn't been able to ignore the rush of envy when she saw women in various stages of confinement with the fathers of their unborn children holding their hands or rubbing their backs. Afterward, she chided herself for being weak and needy.

Wrapping her arms around Sheldon's waist, she rested her cheek over his heart and counted the strong, steady beats. Unbidden tears filled her eyes and overflowed as she cried without making a sound.

Sheldon felt moisture soaking his shirt. He moved his hand over Renee's back in a comforting motion. "Shush, princess. Everything is going to be all right."

His attempt to console made her cry harder and Renee clung to him like a swimmer floundering in a dangerous undertow. She had tried telling herself she could go through nine months of pregnancy and deliver a baby alone, but when she least expected it her armor cracked, revealing her vulnerability and leaving her with a feeling of helplessness.

She pressed a kiss to his strong neck. *Live for today, and let tomorrow take care of itself.* Her mother's mantra echoed in her head. Right now Sheldon had offered her everything she needed for emotional stability. She needed to focus on the present instead of agonizing over whether their relationship would work out in the future.

"I'm ready, Sheldon," she whispered in his ear.

Sheldon froze, his breath stopping in his chest. When it resumed he was certain Renee could feel his heart beating. "Are you certain?"

"Very certain."

Pulling back and staring at her tear-stained face, Sheldon's heart turned over when he saw pleading in her eyes. "I don't want you to come to me because you're feeling vulnerable." His gaze softened. "I can't and won't take advantage of you."

"I am ready," Renee repeated. She pulled her lower lip between her teeth to stop its trembling.

Leaning forward, Renee pressed her mouth to his, kissing, lingering and savoring the taste and touch of his firm mouth. He kissed her back in a series of slow, feathery kisses that set her nerves on edge.

Mouths joined, Sheldon tightened his hold on her body. What had begun as a tender joining segued into a hungry, burning desire, the sparks igniting like brilliant showers of embers flung heavenward. Her sensitive nipples tightened, ached; her breasts grew heavy, swelling against the fabric of her bra.

"Please," she moaned as if in pain.

Sheldon tore his mouth from hers, laser-gray eyes glittering like quicksilver. He knew if he did not stop now he wouldn't be able to. He wanted Renee just that much. His chest rose and fell heavily as if he had run a grueling race.

"Okay, baby. I'll stop." He did not recognize his own voice.

She grabbed the front of his shirt in a punishing grip. Her eyes had darkened with her rising desire. "Don't you dare stop!"

He cradled her head between his large hands. "You know what this means, don't you?" She inclined her head. "If we make love, then there will be no turning back." She nodded again. "Tell me *now* what you want from me."

Renee closed her eyes, shutting out his intense stare. "I want you, Sheldon."

"For what?" he whispered against her lips.

"To protect me and my baby."

He nodded. "I can do that. What else, darling?"

"Become my best friend."

Lowering his head, he nuzzled her neck, inhaling the sensual, haunting scent of Shalimar. "I can do that, too. What else, princess?" Renee opened her eyes and something in her gaze gave Sheldon his answer.

"I want you to be the last man I sleep with."

He swept her off the stool, reached over, turned off the grill and walked out of the kitchen. His long, determined strides took him across the living room, up the staircase and into the bedroom he had never shared with a woman. Whenever he brought a woman to the cabin in the woods they always slept together in one of the first-floor bedrooms. The loft had become his monastery—a private sanctuary—until now.

Shifting Renee's slight weight, he walked to the bed, lowering her to the mattress. The light from the emerging near-full moon cast a silver glow on every light-colored surface. He made his way to the adjoining bath before returning to lie next to her; holding her hand, he stared up at the shadows on the ceiling.

There was only the sound of measured breathing as seconds ticked to minutes. Sheldon pulled her over his chest with a minimum of effort. He met her gaze in the diffused moonlight. "I can make love to you without being inside you."

She willed the tears pricking the back of her eyelids not to fall. Why, she asked herself, did tears come so easily now when in the past she hardly ever cried? Sheldon had scaled the wall she had erected to keep all men out of her life and her heart with a quiet gentleness she hadn't encountered in any man she knew—in or out of bed. He had asked how to proceed because of the child in her womb.

She exhaled audibly. "What I had with Donald is over. Any love I had for him died the moment I walked out of his life. There will never be three people in our bed, and this will be the last time I mention his name to you."

Combing his fingers through her hair, Sheldon cradled her head and kissed her with a passion that threatened to incinerate her. Reversing their positions, he supported his weight on his arms while at the same time he pressed his middle to Renee's, communicating his desire for her.

Slowly, methodically he undressed her, his mouth mapping each inch of flesh he bared. Trailing his tongue over her warm, scented flesh, he committed her smell to memory. The throbbing between his legs increased, yet Sheldon forced himself to go slow, slow enough to give Renee the pleasure he was certain she would wring from him.

The buttons on her blouse gave way and he stared mutely at the swell of flesh spilling over her bra's delicate fabric. Reaching around her back, he released the clasp and slipped off the bra. His breathing quickening, he swallowed a groan. Her breasts were as full and firm as ripe fruit.

Renee felt the heat from Sheldon's gaze as he eased her slacks down her hips and legs. Her panties followed, leaving her naked to his hungry gaze. The pads of his thumbs swept over her swollen nipples, sending pinpoints of exquisite pleasure to the pulsing between her thighs.

Eyes wide, breathing heavily, Sheldon sat back on his heels. "Sweet heaven, princess. You are beautiful," he whispered reverently.

His mouth replaced his hand, suckling her, and she rose off the mattress, her breasts heaving. She wanted to touch Sheldon, taste him the way he was touching and tasting her. Tears filled her eyes again as he lowered his head and trailed soft kisses over her slightly rounded belly. She crooned his name again and again while mouth and tongue worshipped her.

Renee sat up, her hands going to the buttons on his shirt. She managed to undo two, but was thwarted when he brushed her hand aside and accomplished the task in one sweeping motion; buttons were ripped from their fastenings.

Sheldon went to his knees, unsnapped the waistband on his jeans and pulled down the zipper in a motion too quick for the eye to follow. His jeans, briefs and socks lay in a pile with hers on the floor beside the bed.

He slipped the latex sheath over his aroused flesh and extended his arms. He wasn't disappointed when Renee moved into his embrace. Holding her, breathing in her scent, filled him with a sense of completeness. It was as if he had waited twenty years for a little slip of a woman to come into his life, a woman who would change him forever.

Why Renee and not some of the other women he had slept with?

What was so different about her that he had willingly pledged his future to her?

He prayed silently he would discover what it was before he got in too deep.

Supporting his back against the headboard, he cupped Renee's hips, lifting her high enough to straddle his thighs. "Put your legs around my waist." She complied, lowered her forehead to his shoulder, her breath coming in short, quick pants. "Are you comfortable?"

"Yes," she gasped.

All of Renee's tactile senses were on high alert: the mat of chest hair grazing her sensitive breasts, heavy breathing against her ear and the hardness between her thighs. She moaned, then bit down on her lower lip to stifle another one as her flesh stretched to accommodate Sheldon's sex.

She rocked her hips against his, setting the pace. Each push, stroke, moan, groan and gasp of air became part of a dance of desire that sucked them into a vortex of sensual delight that had no beginning, no end.

Renee was drawn to heights of passion she had never known; her body vibrated with the liquid fire scorching her brain and nerve endings. Her lips quivered in the intoxicating desire she had not felt in months.

Sheldon could not stop the groans escaping his parted lips as flames of desire swept over him with the ferocity of a tornado touching down and sweeping up everything in its violent wake. He tried thinking of anything but the woman in his embrace, and failed—miserably.

Cradling her hips, he increased their cadence, their bodies moving faster and faster until the swirling ecstasy escalated and erupted in a tidal wave that swept them away to a private world of erotic enchantment.

Renee collapsed against Sheldon's moist chest, her breath coming in deep surrendering moans. Filled with an amazing sense of completeness, she closed her eyes.

Sheldon loathed having to withdraw from Renee. Their lovemaking had become a raw act of possession. He belonged to her and she belonged to him.

Easing her arms from under his shoulders, he laid her gently on her side before he covered her moist body with a sheet and lightweight blanket. He sat motionless and stared at her, then moved off the bed and made his way to the bathroom.

He stood under the warm spray of the shower recalling what Renee wanted from him. He had been forthcoming when he told her he would protect her and her child. That he'd done with his sons.

However, he knew he could never promise Renee marriage, because despite his success as a father and businessman, he had failed as a husband. That was a failure he would not chance repeating.

Six

Renee lay in the drowsy warmth of the large bed reliving the pleasure and satisfaction she'd shared with Sheldon. His lovemaking—the warmth of his body against hers, his protective embrace and the touch of his lips on hers had left her aching and burning for more.

Even with spiraling ecstasy that had nowhere to go, she'd prayed for it to continue until she was sucked into a vortex that held her prisoner for an eternity.

Reaching over, she turned on a lamp, looking for her clothes. They weren't on the bed or floor. She left the bed and went into the bathroom. The bathroom was more than twice the size of her first apartment. A free-flowing master bath opened into a dressing area with built-in drawers and closets tucked into an alcove. She opened a drawer and took out a T-shirt with the logo of Tuskegee University. Sheldon revealed he had not attended college, and she wondered which of his sons had attended the historically black college.

Opening the cabinets below the vanity, she discovered a plethora of grooming supplies. Twenty minutes later she'd brushed her teeth, showered and moisturized her body. She pulled on the T-shirt, walked out of the bedroom and descended the curving staircase.

Renee hadn't stepped off the last stair when she saw Sheldon, his back to her, setting the table in the dining area. Light from an overhead chandelier created a halo around the damp black hair clinging to his head. He'd changed into a pair of jeans and a black cotton sweater. She smiled. Like her, he had elected to go barefoot.

"Are you certain you don't want my help?"

Turning slowly, Sheldon stared at Renee. She wore the T-shirt Ryan had given him after he'd returned from his alma mater as a visiting professor. The sleeves reached below her elbows and the hem below her knees. His gaze lingered on her shapely legs and bare feet.

A slow smile crinkled his eyes and deepened the slashes in his lean jaw. He moved toward her.

Cradling her face, he dipped his head and brushed a light kiss over her parted lips.

"I'm certain. I wanted to set the table before coming up to get you. Are you hungry?"

She wrinkled her nose and nodded. "Starved. I'm sorry I'm not dressed for dinner, but I couldn't find my clothes."

"I put them in the wash." He kissed her again. "They're now in the dryer." With an arm around her waist, he led Renee to the table. He waited until she'd pulled the hem of the shirt under her hips, then pushed the chair under her.

Sharing dinner with Sheldon was a surreal experience for Renee. He started a fire in the fireplace, dimmed all the lights except in the dining area and tuned on the stereo to a station that featured love songs.

He had prepared a four-course meal beginning with lobster bisque and a salad of tomato and mozzarella topped with freshly grated Parmesan cheese. A grilled steak complemented baked potatoes and blanched snow peas. She'd refused dessert because she had eaten too much at one sitting.

Smiling across the table, she closed her eyes and sighed audibly. "You can cook for me any time."

"Is that what you want me to do? Cook for you?"

Her eyes opened and she sat up straighter. "No, Sheldon. That's not what I want you to do. I wouldn't mind if you cook for me on occasion and I'll do the same for you."

"You cook?"

She affected a frown. "Of course." Her mother had taught her to cook, and by the age of fifteen she could prepare an entire meal by herself.

"No, princess." His voice was low, soothing. "I look forward to cooking for you."

The distinctive voices of Kenny Rogers and Sheena Easton singing "We've Got Tonight" came through speakers hidden throughout the first floor.

Sheldon pushed back his chair, rounded the table and extended his hand to Renee. "Come dance with me. This is one of my favorite songs."

She hesitated. "I can't."

"Why?"

Renee stared over his head rather than meet his questioning gaze. "I don't have on any underwear."

A hint of a smile played around his mobile mouth. "By the time I go and get your underwear the song will be over. But, if you feel uncomfortable, then I'll take off my underwear."

She shot up from the chair and grabbed his hand. "No. Don't. Please."

Sheldon led her out to the middle of the living room, chuckling softly. "I just want you to feel comfortable."

Renee moved into his embrace. "I'm comfortable," she said a little too quickly.

He pulled her close to his body, spinning her around as he sang, "We've got tonight. Who needs tomorrow? Let's make it last."

She closed her eyes, listening to Sheldon sing. Was he saying that he only wanted right now—tonight and not tomorrow?

She wanted to tell Sheldon that tonight was all they had, because tomorrow was not promised. Sinking into his comforting embrace, she rested her head over his heart. The strong, steady beats kept time with hers. The song ended, but they did not pull apart. There was no need for words. Their bodies had communicated without words and what their bodies shared had nothing to do with business.

The clock on the fireplace mantel chimed the half hour as Sheldon and Renee climbed the staircase in the house at Blackstone Farms. It was one-thirty. He'd wanted to stay over until Sunday night, but she complained about having a sore throat.

"I think I'd like to sleep in my own bed."

Sheldon's stoic expression concealed his disappointment. They'd made love but would not sleep together. He nodded. "I'll see you in the morning."

Renee forced a smile. Every time she swallowed she felt as if her throat was on fire. "Good night." Rising on tiptoe, she kissed his cheek. She walked the length of the hallway and into her bedroom. She undressed quickly and slipped into bed.

* * *

Renee woke Sunday morning chilled to the bone. She could not stop her teeth from chattering. It was obvious she had come down with something.

It was ironic that *something* was the reason she'd gotten pregnant. A paralegal at the law firm had died from bacterial meningitis and everyone who had come in contact with her was prescribed a powerful antibiotic. Unknown to Renee, the antibiotic interacted with her low-dose contraceptive, decreasing its potency.

There were times after she'd relocated to Kentucky when she wondered what if Donald hadn't been married. Would he have offered marriage once she told him he was to become a father? The what-ifs had haunted her until she went for a drive, parked along the bank of a small river and screamed at the top of her lungs. The action was enough to purge her what-ifs and lingering angst.

Renee forced herself to leave the bed long enough to brush her teeth and take a hot shower. She made it back to bed on wobbly knees and went back to sleep.

Sheldon walked into the dining hall and saw Jeremy and Tricia sitting at a table with her grandfather, Gus Parker. Tricia motioned for him to join them.

Leaning over, he kissed her cheek. "Good morning."

"Good morning, Pop." Her dark eyes sparkled. "Grandpa has some wonderful news."

Sheldon sat next to his longtime friend. Augustus Parker had come to the farm as a groom two weeks after Sheldon purchased his first thoroughbred, and retired as assistant trainer some thirty years later.

"What's the good news, Gus?"

Tall, thin and nearing eighty, Gus affected a mysterious smile. "I'm getting married." He and his first wife Olga were married for forty-seven years before she died twelve years ago.

Sheldon's shocked expression gave way to a wide grin as he pumped Gus's hand. "Congratulations. Who is the lucky woman?"

"Beatrice Miller."

"Your nurse?" Sheldon asked.

"My ex-nurse and soon-to-be wife."

Tricia rested a hand on her grandfather's shoulder. Gus had suffered a heart attack and been hospitalized in late summer, but had recovered enough to give her away in marriage to Jeremy Blackstone. It was apparent the middle-aged visiting nurse not only helped heal the older man's heart; she'd softened it as well.

"When is the big day, Grandpa?"

"I'm leaving that up to Beatrice."

"Do you plan to move off the farm?" Sheldon asked.

Gus shook his head. "No. I wouldn't even consider leaving now that I'm going to become a great-grandfather." He winked at his granddaughter. "Beatrice told me she would love to fill in for Tricia as school nurse once she goes out on maternity leave."

Tricia stared at Gus. "I'm not going out on maternity leave, Grandpa. The baby is due the first week in July. School is over by that time. I'll have two months to bond with the baby, then I'll see it every day at the school's infant center."

Sheldon thought about Renee and her baby. She'd told him she was in her fourth month, which meant she would probably deliver sometime in March. Although she would not have worked for Blackstone Farms long enough to make her eligible for maternity leave, he would ask Jeremy to allow her some time off.

He glanced down at his watch. It was nearly noon and Renee had not put in an appearance. If she did not come to the dining hall before he'd left it, he would bring her breakfast favorites to the house.

Sheldon rapped on Renee's bedroom door, listening for movement on the other side. He tried the knob, turning it slowly. The door opened silently and he walked over to the bed. She lay on her side, eyes closed. He touched a bare shoulder, then jerked his hand away. She was burning up!

Guilt attacked him. He thought she'd refused to share his bed because she hadn't felt comfortable sleeping with him at the farm. Reaching for the cell phone on his waistband, he dialed Jeremy's number. The call was answered after the second ring.

"Tell Tricia I need her to come and check on

Renee. She's burning up with fever." Ending the call, Sheldon walked into the bathroom, wet a towel with cold water, then retraced his steps.

Jeremy and Tricia found Sheldon sitting on the side of Renee's bed, dabbing her face and neck with a cloth.

Tricia met her father-in-law's worried gaze. "Let me take her temperature."

Sheldon rose from the bed. He stood with his back to the window, watching intently as Tricia took Renee's temperature and blood pressure.

"Last night she complained of a sore throat," he said in a quiet voice.

Tricia glanced at Sheldon over her shoulder. "At least half a dozen kids have also come down with sore throats. The doctor tested them for streptococcus."

A frown appeared between Sheldon's eyes. "Did any of them have it?"

"No. All of the cultures came back negative."

"I can't take antibiotics," Renee said in a croaking voice.

Tricia met her gaze. "Why not?"

Renee closed her eyes. It hurt her to talk or swallow. "I'm pregnant."

Jeremy and Tricia turned and stared at Sheldon, whose impassive expression did not change with Renee's admission. They exchanged a knowing look. It was apparent the elder Blackstone knew about Renee's condition.

"I want her tested for strep throat," Sheldon ordered softly.

After tucking her stereoscope and blood pressure equipment into a small black leather case Tricia stood up. "You want the doctor to come out here today?"

"Call him, Tricia. *Now.*" Sheldon could barely control his annoyance. The farm's on-call physician was paid a generous retainer to come at a moment's notice.

Jeremy was more than familiar with his father's explosive temper. He had challenged him countless times as an adolescent, and had always come up the loser.

"I'll call the doctor, Pop." Turning on his heels, Jeremy walked out of Renee's bedroom.

Tricia, more than anxious to follow her husband, said, "Make certain she drinks lots of water to avoid dehydration. I'll wait downstairs for Dr. Gibson."

Renee lost track of time, but she remembered hearing the doctor tell Sheldon she had contracted a virus, and with bed rest, a light diet and plenty of fluids she should feel better in three to five days.

She slept for hours, waking to find Sheldon hovering over her while urging her to drink from the glass he held to her lips. Milk and blended fruity concoctions were added; these she sipped through a straw. What she did not remember was Sheldon washing her body as if she were a small, helpless child. Early one morning she woke up to find him asleep on the chair in the sitting room.

* * *

Renee sat up in bed Tuesday afternoon alert and ravenous. The first thing she noticed was that she wasn't wearing a nightgown, but a man's T-shirt; the second was the woman coming out of the bathroom with a pail filled with cleaning supplies. Even though she'd met Claire Garrett at the pre-race party, she'd only seen the housekeeper once before. She heard the hum of her vacuum cleaner, but failed to catch a glimpse of the tall elusive woman.

The third thing she noticed was the most shocking: her stomach. She'd lost her waistline the month before, leaving her belly slightly rounded; however, now it protruded above her pelvis.

Claire smiled, her bright green eyes sparkling like emeralds. "I'll let Sheldon know you're up."

"Thank you." The two words came out in a low husky tone. Her throat no longer hurt, but whatever she'd picked up had affected her vocal cords.

Renee returned Claire's smile as she swung her legs over the side of the bed. Her feet touched the cool bare floor and she shivered. It wasn't even winter and she felt cold. It probably would take her some time to get used to the change of seasons.

Walking into the bathroom, she filled the tub with water, added a capful of bath salts, the scent of vanilla wafting in the air. She brushed her teeth, rinsed her mouth with a mint-flavored mouthwash and washed her face, then stepped into the tub. Sighing, she rested her head on a bath pillow and closed her eyes.

"Do you need me to wash your back?"

Sitting up and splashing water over the sides of tub, Renee spied Sheldon lounging in the doorway, smiling broadly. A swath of heat cut a path from her face to her toes.

"No…no thank you."

Sheldon could not move, not even to breathe. The sight of her full breasts and the timbre of her husky voice rendered him temporarily paralyzed. The increasing heaviness between his thighs was akin to pain, a pain he did not want to go away.

"Does your throat still hurt?"

Sinking lower in the water, she shook her head. "No. But I sound like a foghorn."

He fixed his stare on her dewy face, smiling. "All foghorns should sound so sexy."

Sheldon knew he had to leave the bathroom *now,* or he would strip off his clothes and join Renee in the bathtub. "I'll see you downstairs."

He knew his feelings for the woman living under his roof were intensifying with every minute he remained in her presence. Sitting and watching Renee sleep while he waited for her body to heal had taken him back twenty years. Then he'd sat by another woman's bedside, waiting and watching her die. While the events in his life had changed in two decades, he hadn't—not until now.

In the past, he'd slept with other women because of sexual frustration. However, it was different with Renee because he did not need her as much as he wanted her. A wry smile tilted the corners of his mouth. It was time he opened himself to accept whatever life offered.

Seven

"Is this your first one?"

Sheldon pulled his gaze away from *The Washington Post* and looked at the red-haired man sitting on his right. A slight frown furrowed his smooth forehead. "First what?"

"Baby?"

His frown vanished. "No."

"Which one is it?"

As promised, Sheldon had accompanied Renee to her obstetrician the following week.

"This one will be the tenth," Sheldon replied, deadpan.

The man's face paled, leaving a sprinkling of

freckles over his nose and cheeks before a bright pink flush eased its way up from his neck to forehead. "You're kiddin', dude?"

Nodding and hoping not to burst into laughter, Sheldon continued the charade. "Nope. I have nine sons. We keep trying because we're hoping for a girl."

"Holy…" The redhead's words trailed off.

Sheldon went back to reading his newspaper.

Renee walked into the waiting room at the same time he finished reading the business section. He placed the newspaper on a coffee table and rose to his feet. Her dimpled smile was as bright as a spotlight.

When she had come to Blackstone Farms he never would have suspected she was carrying a baby. Now three weeks later, a hint of a belly was apparent under her khaki-colored tunic.

He closed the distance between them, putting an arm around her waist. "How are you?"

She snuggled closer to his side, her arms circling his waist. "Wonderful. It's a girl!"

Lowering his head, Sheldon pressed a kiss to her forehead. "Congratulations."

The moment she had informed him she was pregnant and intended to raise her child alone he'd hoped for a girl. He'd been a single father, and there were times when his teenage sons tested the limits of his patience *and* sanity.

He'd found girls quieter, less aggressive than boys. The difference between his three-month-old granddaughter Vivienne and Sean at the same age was like night and day. Vivienne was content to coo and play with her fingers and toes, while Sean had demanded to be picked up whenever he wasn't sleeping.

"When's your next appointment?"

"A month from now."

"Is everything okay?"

"I'm fine, Sheldon. Let's get out of here," Renee said quietly. Seeing some of the women in their last days of confinement was a blatant indicator of what awaited her.

Sheldon escorted Renee through the waiting area, stopping only to tap the inquisitive man on his shoulder. "We can stop now. It's a girl."

He glared up at Sheldon. "What if it was going to be another boy?"

Leaning closer, his gray eyes giving off sparks like streaks of lightning, Sheldon bared his straight white teeth. "Then I'd keep trying, *dude*."

Waiting until they were out in the parking lot, Renee placed a hand on Sheldon's arm. "Did I miss something back in the doctor's office?"

Sheldon opened the pickup's passenger-side door. "He asked me how many children I had and I told him nine." He bit back a smile when Renee's delicate jaw dropped. "I said we were going to keep trying until we got a girl."

Resting her hands on his chest, Renee shook her head. "You're bad, Sheldon Blackstone."

He moved closer, trapping her between his body and the truck's door. "How bad, princess?"

Tilting her chin, she stared up at him through her lashes. "Very, very bad, your highness."

Sheldon dipped his head. "Is that a good bad or a bad bad?"

Closing her eyes against his intense stare, she shook her head. "I don't know." The sultry hoarseness in her voice floated around them like a low, lingering fog.

"What would I have to do to help you make up your mind?"

Renee opened her eyes. "I'll leave that to your imagination."

Without warning, she found herself swept up in a strong embrace and seated in the truck. She did not have time to catch her breath when Sheldon got in beside her, put the vehicle in gear and drove out of the parking lot.

"Where are you going?" Renee asked as Sheldon parked the truck behind a gourmet shop.

Leaning over, he kissed her cheek. "How would you like to share a late afternoon picnic dinner with me?"

She ran the tip of her tongue over her lower lip, drawing his gaze to linger there. "Where?"

He raised an eyebrow. "Front porch, back porch, your bedroom or mine. It's your call."

Renee thought of his choices, then said, "How about outdoors?" The early frost had come and gone, and the Indian summer temperatures topped out in the low seventies during the daytime hours.

Sheldon regarded Renee for a minute. She was totally unpredictable, a trait he liked because he knew she would never bore him. "Outdoors it is."

Renee lay on a blanket in the same spot where she'd lain with Sheldon on Halloween. They sampled the most delectable foods, emptied a bottle of sparkling water, then fell asleep in each other's arms.

The sun had begun its descent and the air had cooled considerably when she stirred, her face pressed to Sheldon's solid chest, one leg sandwiched between his.

"Sheldon?"

He opened his eyes at her sultry query. "Yes, baby?"

"I want you to be bad."

There was a pulse beat of silence. "How bad?"

There came another pause. "Naughty."

Cradling her body with one arm, Sheldon rolled Renee over on her back. "Here?"

She nodded. "Yes."

"I can't protect you, because I didn't bring any condoms with me."

Renee giggled like a little girl. "It's too late for that, Sheldon. Remember, I'm already pregnant."

She was pregnant and he was disease-free. He had used a condom with her the first time because he didn't want Renee to think he was cavalier when it came to sleeping with women.

Sitting back on his heels, he reached down and pulled off his waffle-knit pullover. His gaze fused and locked with Renee's as he removed boots, jeans and boxers. He followed her gaze as it moved downward.

The first time they'd made love it had been in the silvered glow of a full moon, and now it was in the fading shadows of the setting sun. He had tasted and touched her like a sightless man, but this time everything she claimed would be presented for his viewing.

A cool breeze rustled the leaves on an overhead tree, leaves falling and littering the blanket like colorful confetti. Shifting, Sheldon removed Renee's shoes and striped trouser socks. He unbuttoned her tunic, his breath catching in his chest. Leaning over, he pressed a kiss to her distended belly.

"You're beautiful, princess."

Renee closed her eyes. "I'm fat, Sheldon."

Reaching for her hand, he placed it over her stomach. "You're filled with life, darling. Don't you realize how special that is?"

She opened her eyes, seeing unspoken pain glowing in his eyes and recalling the loved ones he'd buried. "Yes." Her voice was barely a whisper. "This baby is special."

He removed her tunic, bra and panties with a skill and familiarity indicating he had performed the action innumerable times.

Renee did not have time to ponder his statement when she found herself naked to his penetrating gaze.

Extending her arms, she welcomed Sheldon into her embrace. She did not feel the full effect of his comforting weight because he'd supported it on his arms.

Under a darkening autumn sky with all of nature as their audience, they began a dance of desire that needed no dress rehearsal.

His eyes smoldering with liquid fire, Sheldon feasted on the woman who made him look forward to the next day, the woman who made him laugh without trying to be funny and the woman who made him want to be inside her every day, hour, minute, second.

He brushed featherlike kisses around her mouth. Her lips parted of their own volition, and his tongue entwined with hers like pieces of molten steel. He did not kiss her mouth, but devoured it before moving down to the scented column of her neck, lingering at the base of her throat.

Traveling southward, he tasted one breast, then the other. She gasped as if in pain and rose off the blanket when his teeth closed on a nipple, worrying it gently before giving the other equal attention.

Renee was mindless with the divine ecstasy wrung from her. The pulsing between her legs thrummed faster, harder, and she was afraid it would be over before he claimed her body. She reached for his hair, fingers tightening in the heavy strands.

"Please do it, Sheldon," she begged hoarsely. "Take me, *now!*"

He complied, easing his sex into her warm, pulsing flesh. The turbulence of her passion swept Sheldon up in a flood tide of the hottest fire, clouding his brain. He was lost in the flames threatening to devour not just a part of him, but all that he was and he had hoped to become.

Then it came upon him like the whispered feet of a cat out of the darkness of the night. Feelings, emotions, sensations he had locked away when he'd buried Julia surfaced. The love he'd had for one woman, the love he was unable to offer another, trickled through the chasm in his heart, bursting forth, rushing and sweeping him up in its turbulent wake of realization as he surrendered all to the woman in his arms.

Renee welcomed the powerful thrusts, meeting each one with her own. Her hands were everywhere: in his hair, trembling over his broad shoulders, tunneling through the thick mat of hair on his chest. She wanted to yield to the burning sweetness that held her prisoner, but knew it was only a matter of seconds before she was forced to surrender to the raging passion lifting her higher and higher until she floated beyond herself. Her breath came in long, surrendering moans, and she gave in to the ecstasy.

The sounds escaping Renee's parted lips became Sheldon's undoing. Lowering his head, he growled in her ear as the explosions erupted in his lower body. The aftermath left him gasping and fighting for his next breath. It was a full two minutes before he was able to move, collapsing heavily to the blanket.

Renee rolled over on her side and rested her head on his shoulder. He pulled her close, offering his body's heat. "Don't go to sleep on me, darling," he whispered in her hair.

"I can't move."

"You don't have to."

Renee lay motionless while Sheldon pulled on his clothes, then dressed her. During the short ride to the house, she managed to doze off. It wasn't until hours later that she remembered sharing a shower with Sheldon and his request to share her bed.

Around three o'clock she woke up and made her way downstairs for a glass of milk. She returned to the bedroom, finding Sheldon sitting up and waiting for her. There was no mistaking the concern in his gaze.

"Are you all right?"

Renee got into bed, straddled his lap, wiggling until she found a comfortable position. "I just went down to get a glass of milk."

"You shouldn't do that," he crooned in her ear.

"Do what?"

"Sit on me."

A sensual smile touched her mouth. "And why not?"

"Because you'll find yourself on your back and me inside you…"

Her explosive kiss cut off his words. It was her

turn to gasp as Sheldon gathered the hem of her nightgown, pushing it above her waist. He lifted her with one arm and joined their bodies, making them one.

Instinctively, her body arched toward him. The crisp chest hair teased and tantalized her sensitive nipples and she welcomed the erotic sensation. Writhing, she moved closer, rocking up and down, back and forth over his hardness. Why, she asked herself as she came down to meet Sheldon in a moment of uncontrolled passion, couldn't she get enough of him? What spell had he cast over her that made her temporarily forget everything—even her name?

Sated, she collapsed against Sheldon, her lower lip trembling from the ebbing raw sensuality coursing through her. She did not know if the increase in her libido was from her being pregnant or from the realization that she was falling in love with Sheldon Blackstone.

In the six weeks Renee lived at Blackstone Farms, she had changed. The most apparent change was her body. Anyone who saw her knew she was carrying a child, and despite Sheldon's reassurance that he found her more beautiful than when she'd first come to the farm, there were times when she felt clumsy and misshapen.

Since they'd begun sleeping together it was always in her bed, because despite their intimacy she felt something was missing in their relationship.

Each time she opened her arms to Sheldon the love she felt for him deepened. Each time he brought her to the pinnacle of desire she feared blurting out how much she had come to love him.

She had asked Sheldon for friendship, a confidant; his proposition included companionship and a promise to protect her and her child. Falling in love was not a part of their agreement—that went beyond business.

Late the next afternoon Renee mounted the porch, opened the door and walked into the main house. Heat greeted her as she went through the entryway and up the staircase.

The door to Sheldon's bedroom was slightly ajar and she heard him singing loudly. A knowing smile softened Renee's vermilion-colored lips as she walked to her bedroom. At first she'd found it odd that although she and Sheldon lived together, they rarely encountered each other during the day. It was only at night whenever Sean did not come for a sleep-over with his grandfather that they slept together.

A strapless periwinkle-blue silk gown with an empire waist and slip lay across the bed; the matching quilted jacket hung from a padded hanger in the armoire.

Twenty minutes later Renee slipped her feet into a pair of sapphire-blue silk heels and walked over to the full-length mirror on the door of armoire. She did not recognize the woman staring back at her. Her hair had been pulled off her face and pinned into a chignon at the back of her head. The style was sophisticated without being too severe.

A slight gasp escaped her as another image joined hers in the mirror. Sheldon stood behind her, resplendent in formal dress. He wore a tailored tuxedo, white spread collar dress shirt and dark blue silk tie with an aplomb she hadn't seen on many men. Close-cropped raven hair brushed off his forehead and fell in layered precision against his scalp. The heat from his body and the tantalizing smell of his aftershave made her heart beat a little too quickly.

Sheldon placed one hand over the silk fabric artfully concealing her belly; the other circled her neck. His thumb caressed the skin over the nape of her neck as Renee's gaze met his.

His impassive expression did not reveal what he was feeling at that moment, what lay in his heart. He had deliberately avoided Renee because he'd found himself caught in a web of desire that held him captive. Each time he encountered her he was sucked into a force field, making him helpless and vulnerable. These were familiar emotions he had not wanted to experience again.

Renee shivered as Sheldon's forefinger toyed with the diamond stud in her right ear. Closing her eyes, she rested her head against his shoulder. The shiver became a noticeable shudder as he trailed kisses along the column of her neck.

"You look incredibly beautiful, smell delicious and taste scrumptious," he murmured against her velvety flesh.

Renee drank in his strength. "If we don't leave now, we're going to be late," she said not too convincingly.

"We won't be late, princess," he whispered, nuzzling her ear. "Thank you, darling."

She melted against his stronger body, her breath coming quickly. "For what, honey?" The endearment slipped out of its own accord.

"For being you, Renee." Sheldon's hands went to her upper arms and he turned her in his embrace. His hands came up and he cradled her face. His gaze widened, the gray orbs missing nothing. "I never thought you'd be able to improve on perfection, but you have. I'm going to be the envy of every man tonight." Her professionally coiffed hair and makeup highlighted her best features.

Renee reached for his hands, pulling them down. "Is that why you asked me to go with you and paid for this dress? To show me off like one of your prize thoroughbreds?"

A warning cloud settled into Sheldon's features, his expression a mask of stone. "Is that what you think, Renee?"

"Yes."

He shook his head slowly. "You don't know, do you?"

Her waxed eyebrows lifted. "Know what?"

Without warning his expression changed, his eyes brimming with tenderness and passion. "I adore you."

Renee's body stiffened in shock, complete surprise on her face. Sheldon had given her everything she wanted, but she never suspected deeper feelings would become a part of their plan. She wanted to tell Sheldon she adored and loved him, too, but his confession caused the words to wedge in her throat.

"Thank you," she whispered, recovering her voice.

Inclining his head, Sheldon forced a smile, successfully concealing his disappointment. It was apparent she did not share his sentiment.

Threads of doubt nagged at him. Was she still in love with her ex?

"Are you ready?"

She nodded. "Yes."

Eight

Renee walked out of the chapel, her hand resting on Sheldon's sleeve. She had given him several sidelong glances as the bride and groom exchanged vows, wondering whether he had relived the moment when he'd married his young bride; however, his solemn expression had not changed.

Sheldon covered the small hand on his arm. Renee's fingers were ice-cold. "Are you all right?"

"Yes. Why?"

"Your hand feels cold."

"This is one time when I'm not cold." The temperature inside the mansion was comfortably set for the expanse of bared skin in low-cut and backless gowns.

The number of carats glittering from throats, wrists and ears of the other women present in the grand ballroom stunned Renee. The guests were Virginia's aristocracy, with a few Washington senators and other politicians in attendance. The wedding was touted as the wedding of the year, linking heirs to two of the largest and the most profitable horse farms in the state.

Sheldon found their table and seated her. Leaning down, he pressed his mouth to her ear. "What can I get you to drink?" Guests were quickly lining up at several bars set up around the ballroom.

Renee opened her mouth to say milk, but changed her mind. "Sparkling water with a wedge of lime."

Sheldon chuckled softly, his gaze straying from her mouth to the swell of breasts rising and falling above her revealing décolletage. "Does this mean that I'm going to have to be the designated driver tonight?"

"Hello again, Renee." A familiar voice interrupted their interchange.

Renee glanced over her shoulder. Kent Taylor leered at her chest, a lopsided grin on his face. His attention was temporarily averted when Sheldon grabbed his hand and shook it, while pounding his back.

"When are you racing Kiss Me Kate again?"

The high color in Kent's face deepened. He still had not recovered from his horse coming in second at the International Gold Cup. "I don't know." He eased his fingers from Sheldon's firm grip. "I hope you don't mind if I ask your lady for a dance later on tonight."

Sheldon's cold smile would've chilled most men, but Kent was too inebriated to notice. "I do mind."

Nonplussed, Kent blinked a few times, hoping he hadn't heard what he thought he heard. Shrugging a shoulder, he turned and walked away.

"He's worse than a swarm of mosquitoes," Sheldon mumbled under his breath.

Renee's eyes narrowed. "I hope you're not going to growl at every man who asks to dance with me. I came here tonight to have a good time."

Sheldon hunkered down beside her chair, cradled the back of her head and pressed his mouth to hers. "And you will have a good time."

Her dimples winked at him. "You promise."

His smile matched hers. "I promise."

She did have a good time as she danced with Sheldon. A band whose repertoire included more than four decades of familiar tunes replaced a string quartet that played during the meal and many toasts.

Excusing herself, Renee whispered to Sheldon that she was going to the ladies' lounge. Making her way across the marble floor of the ballroom, she felt as if every eye was directed at her. Whenever Sheldon introduced her, he only offered her first name. Of course that made her more mysterious and others more curious.

Fortunately, she did not have to wait on line in the opulent bath and powder room. In the stall, as she adjusted her dress, she heard someone mention her name.

"Who is she?" came a soft drawling female voice.

"I don't know." This feminine voice was lower, more dulcet than the other woman's. "I thought you knew who she was. After all, you went to Sheldon's pre-race party."

"I don't remember her," the first woman admitted in a hushed tone.

"Where on earth do you think Sheldon picked her up?"

"I don't know. Maybe he joined some dating service, or he could've picked her up in one of those so-called gentlemen's clubs. You can find anything there."

"What do you mean anything?"

"Women who dance topless and swing around poles."

"Are you saying she's a whore?"

"She doesn't really look like a whore. But, one can never tell nowadays."

"The cut of her dress is a little deceiving, but I think she's in the family way."

"Bite your tongue, Valerie Marie Winston. I can't imagine Sheldon waiting until he's a grandfather to start making babies again."

"Bite your own tongue, Susanna Caroline Sullivan.

You see what she looks like. The good Lord was certainly smiling on her when He handed out bosoms."

Renee could not move. If she left the stall, then the women would know she was eavesdropping on their conversation. But she also did not intend to hide behind the door indefinitely.

"No one has seen Sheldon with a woman since Julia died. Maybe he was having a problem with you-know-what," Valerie continued.

"Where have you been?" Susanna chided. "There are drugs for men with that kind of *problem.*"

Renee had heard enough. Sliding back the lock, she left the stall. The shocked expression on the women's faces was priceless. It was impossible to tell their ages. They were the surgically altered women Sheldon had mentioned: perfect noses, collagen-enhanced lips, facelifts and expertly dyed ash-blond hair.

Smiling, she washed her hands and accepted a towel from the bathroom attendant. It was apparent Valerie and Susanna thought the woman so insignificant they could gossip in her presence. Opening her evening purse, she left a bill in the plate on the countertop before she faced the elegantly dressed women who had taken a sudden interest in powdering their noses.

Renee cradled her breasts, her gaze meeting and fusing with wide-eyed stares in the mirror. "Yes, these are mine. And to set the record straight, Sheldon Blackstone doesn't have that particular *problem.*"

Head held high, back ramrod-straight, Renee

strutted out of the rest room, staring down anyone whose gaze lingered longer than was sociably polite.

She found Sheldon sitting with several men as she neared their table. Vertical lines appeared between his eyes when he saw her tight-lipped expression. He stood up, the other men following suit.

Rounding the table, Sheldon cupped Renee's elbow. "What's wrong?"

"I want to leave," she whispered.

"Now?"

Renee had clenched her teeth so tightly that her jaw ached. "Yes, Sheldon. Now."

Sheldon saw something in Renee's eyes that had never been there before, and he wondered what had set her off. He nodded to the other men. "Gentlemen. We'll continue our conversation another time."

"Give me a call next week, Blackstone, so we can get together."

"Will do," Sheldon said to a tall, lanky man who bore an uncanny resemblance to Abraham Lincoln.

He led Renee out of the ballroom and retrieved her jacket from the cloakroom. They waited, staring at each other in silence while a valet brought his car around.

Five minutes into the return drive to the farm, Sheldon broke the swollen silence. "What's the matter, Renee?" She told him everything, including the full names of the two women who had indirectly called her a whore.

"If this is a taste of what I'm going to have to confront every time we go out together, then I want out of our agreement. They know nothing about me, yet they have the audacity to call me a whore."

Signaling, Sheldon maneuvered the car to the shoulder of the road and stopped. He shifted into park. His eyes glittered like particles of diamond dust in the diffused light of the dashboard. "You know who you are, and I know who—"

"You know nothing about me," Renee countered, cutting him off. "You've slept with me, Sheldon, yet you know nothing about me." She willed the tears filling her eyes not to fall.

His eyes widened. "Is what you've told me about yourself a lie?" he asked in a dangerously soft voice.

Averting her head, she stared out the windshield. The rapid pumping of her heart echoed in her ears, the roaring sound deafening. "When you introduced me to your high-born *friends* why didn't you give my full name? I'm not on the FBI's Most Wanted list. I'm also not one of those women who make their living as Amber or Bambi for 1-900-talk-dirty-to-me."

Sheldon shook his head. "It's not like that, darling."

"Oh, really? Let me tell you what it's like. I'm not going out with you again."

Sheldon gave Renee a long, penetrating stare. She did not understand, couldn't understand her impact on those who'd met her. The men were awed by her lush beauty, the women envious because she claimed what most of them hadn't had in a long time—natural beauty. He would not refute her accusations. Not now. Not when she was so visibly upset. He shifted into gear, then rejoined the flow of traffic.

He didn't know whether Renee had lied to him about her ex, but he was certain of one thing: he hadn't been entirely forthcoming when he admitted adoring her. The truth was that he *had* fallen in *love* with her. It was only the second time in his life that he'd found himself in love with a woman.

Renee sat at the workstation, staring out the window instead of printing an inventory schedule. She hadn't been able to concentrate for days. Her confrontation with Sheldon had caused a shift in her emotional equilibrium.

They'd returned home Saturday night, climbed the staircase and gone to bed—alone. She hadn't seen or heard from him in days, and it was over breakfast she overheard Ryan tell Jeremy that they would have to wait for Sheldon to return from his mountain retreat.

He had gone without her, and his promise to teach her to fish had been an empty one.

She felt a familiar flutter, closed her eyes and smiled. Her expanding waistline, viewing sonogram pictures and listening to the rapidly beating heartbeat with Doppler had all become insignificant since the first time she felt her baby move.

"Renee."

She swiveled on her chair. Jeremy stood in the doorway. He had come for his report. "Please come in. I just have to print out the schedule for you."

Jeremy sat in a chair near a desk, draping one leg over the opposite knee and studied Renee from under lowered lids. She'd changed since coming to the farm, and it wasn't only the changes in her body. She had become less reclusive, more open with the other farm residents.

He'd told himself to mind his own business; what went on between Sheldon and Renee was of no concern of his. The responsibility of running the horse farm, being a husband and impending fatherhood left little time for him to indulge in gossip.

Leaning forward, Jeremy studied the printed list Renee had tacked to a corkboard. It was a schedule of tasks and projected dates for completion. So far, it appeared as if she was ahead of schedule.

While Renee waited for the printer to complete printing more than thirty sheets, her cell phone rang. The sound startled her. It wasn't often her phone rang, and if it did it was usually her mother, brother or sister-in-law.

Reaching for the tiny instrument, she pushed the talk button. "Hello."

"Hey, Rennie."

She smiled. It was her brother. "Hey, yourself. What's up, Teddy?"

There was a pause before Edward Wilson's voice came through the earpiece. "This is not a social call, Rennie."

Knees shaking, she sank down to her chair and closed her eyes. "Is it Mama?" She had just spoken to her mother the week before.

"No," came his quick reply. "It's about Donald."

Renee sat up straighter, opened her eyes. "What about him?"

"He called here looking for you. He said he just got a divorce and he wants to marry you."

"What did you tell him?"

"I told him that I didn't know where you were."

"Thanks, Teddy."

"Don't thank me yet, Rennie. He says he knows you always spend Thanksgiving with us, so he plans to stop by to see if he can run into you."

"I can't come, Teddy. If he sees me then he'll know that I'm carrying his baby." Her voice had lowered when a pair of smoky gray eyes studied her.

"Then, don't come. Let me handle Mr. Rush. If he decides to get funky with me, then I'll just have to lock him up. I'll come up with a charge after I cuff the lying bastard."

Renee smiled. Her brother, a Kentucky state trooper, flew into a rage after she'd told him of Donald's duplicity.

"I'm going to miss you guys."

"We'll miss you, too. Let's plan to get together for

Christmas. I have a lot of time coming to me, so we'll come to Virginia. The kids have been bugging me about visiting Williamsburg."

"I would like to see it, too."

"Then that does it. We'll come by and pick you up Friday afternoon, and bring you back Monday night."

"Okay, Teddy."

"I'll call and let you know if the clown shows up here."

Renee pulled her lower lip between her teeth. "Please be careful. I've seen Donald lose his temper a few times and he was unbelievably rude."

"Don't worry about me. You just stay put."

"Okay. Love you, Teddy."

"Love you back, Rennie."

Renee ended the call, gathering the pages from the printer. She stapled and handed them to Jeremy, mindful her hands were shaking.

Jeremy took the papers without dropping his gaze. "Do you want to get together when you're feeling better?"

"I'm all right," she said a little too quickly.

"You're shaking."

"I'll be okay in a few minutes." She made her way over to her chair and sat down. Meeting her boss's questioning gaze, Renee drew in a deep breath before letting it out slowly. "The first page is an analysis covering the past three years."

Jeremy half listened to what Renee was saying, his mind recalling her telephone conversation. He knew Teddy was her brother, because when he'd called the Louisville area code and exchange, Teddy Wilson had answered the call, telling him he would give his sister the message.

He hadn't intended to eavesdrop on her conversation, but once she said, *"If he sees me then he'll know that I'm carrying his baby,"* all of his senses were on full alert. It was obvious Renee did not want the father of her baby to know her whereabouts.

There came a light knock against the door frame. "I'm sorry for interrupting." Jeremy and Renee turned to find Sheldon's broad shoulders filling out the doorway. He nodded to her. "Good afternoon."

Renee hadn't realized how much she'd missed Sheldon until now. She missed his drawling voice, deep sensual laugh and most of all the warmth of his embrace. She had come to depend on him more than she'd wanted to.

Tilting her chin, she smiled up at him. "Good afternoon, Sheldon."

Jeremy studied the myriad of emotions crossing Sheldon's face. His mother had died the year he turned ten; however, he'd been old enough to recognize the surreptitious glances between his parents. Unspoken glances that precipitated retiring to bed before their sons. And the look his father and Renee shared was one usually reserved for lovers.

Sheldon reluctantly pulled his gaze away from Renee and nodded at his son. "Jeremy."

"Hey, Pop. I'm glad you're back because I need to talk to you."

"I'll be in the den when you're finished here."

Jeremy turned to Renee. "Can we finish this another time?"

She blinked as if coming out a trance. "Of course."

Jeremy stood up and followed Sheldon, the remnants of Renee's conversation with her brother lingering in his head.

Sheldon entered the den and sat in his favorite chair, while Jeremy took a facing love seat. "What's up?"

Jeremy studied his father, seeing what he would look like in another twenty years, while hoping he would age as elegantly.

"Ryan and Kevin want to race Jahan at Santa Anita and Kentucky Oaks."

Leaning forward and clasping his hands between his knees, Sheldon caught and held Jeremy's gaze. "You don't trust their decision?"

"It's not that I don't trust them, Pop. It's just that I—"

"You don't trust them, Jeremy," Sheldon repeated emphatically, interrupting his younger son. "If you did then we wouldn't be having this conversation. Once I retired and turned complete control of running the farm to you, I'd hoped you wouldn't second-guess Ryan or Kevin's decision whether a horse is ready for a race.

"When you and Ryan decided to race Jahan for the International Gold Cup, I conceded because you, Kevin and Ryan overruled me by three-to-one. You've been overruled, Jeremy, so leave it at that."

For a long moment, Jeremy stared back at Sheldon. "Okay, Pop. I won't oppose them. But, there is something else I should tell you."

He repeated what he'd heard of Renee's conversation with her brother, watching Sheldon change before his eyes like a snake shedding its skin. An expression of hardness had transformed his father into someone he did not know—a stranger.

It was Jeremy's turn to lean forward. "Talk to me, Pop."

Sheldon's voice was low, quiet as he told his son what Renee had disclosed about her relationship with Donald Rush. "Are you familiar with the slug?" he asked.

"I know he is a pioneer in the computer game industry."

"Like those games Sean plays with?"

Jeremy nodded. "Yes. She doesn't want him to find her, Pop."

"And he won't. At least not here. If he steps one foot on Blackstone property he'll be shot on sight."

"What are you going to do? Hold her hostage?"

Sheldon shook his head. "No. I'll protect her. I want you to increase security around the property."

"Can you actually protect Renee from a man who

might sue for joint custody of a child he can prove is his?"

"No," Sheldon admitted.

"I know another way you can protect Renee without becoming her bodyguard or shooting her ex-boyfriend."

"How?"

Jeremy watched his father with hooded eyes that resembled a hawk. "Marry her." The instant the two words were uttered, he girded himself for a violent outburst, but when Sheldon sat staring at him with eyes filled with raw, unspoken pain he regretted the suggestion.

Lowering his head, Sheldon stared at the toes of his boots. "I can't do that."

"Why not, Pop?"

His head came up. "Why not?" he repeated. "Because I wouldn't be a good husband for her."

"Is it because she's carrying another man's baby?"

"No. I wouldn't have a problem raising her child as my own."

"Then, what is it?"

A melancholy frown flitted across Sheldon's taut features. "I wasn't there for Julia when she needed me. Your mother found a lump in her breast, and had a biopsy without my knowledge; when she discovered it was malignant she swore her doctor to secrecy."

Jeremy's eyes widened. "Why wouldn't she tell you?"

"Because she knew I never would've completed the circuit for Boo-yaw's Derby eligibility. She knew how much I wanted a Derby win."

"But, Pop. You can't blame yourself for something you couldn't control."

Sheldon buried his face in his hands. "The signs were there, son, but I was too caught up in my own world to notice them."

Moving to the opposite end of the love seat, Jeremy rested a hand on his father's shoulder. "What happened with my mother is over, and can't be undone. But now you have a second chance to make things right."

Sheldon's head jerked up. "What are you talking about?"

Rising to his feet, Jeremy turned to walk out of the room. He hesitated, but didn't turn around. "Look at what you have, and what you could hope to have."

Sheldon repeated Jeremy's cryptic statement to himself, refusing to accept the obvious. The minutes ticked off, the afternoon shadows lengthened, the sun dipped lower on the horizon. Dusk had fallen when he finally left the den.

Nine

Renee did not see the shadowy figure sitting on the top stair until she was practically on top of him. If she hadn't been daydreaming then she would have detected the familiar fragrance of sandalwood aftershave.

The telephone call from her brother had continued to haunt her although she'd told herself over and over that Donald wouldn't come after her. After all, she was just one in a string of many women he had dated or lived with—one of a lot of foolish women who thought they could hope to become Mrs. Donald Rush.

The only difference between her and Donald's

other women was that it had taken him more than a year to get her to agree to go out with him. And once she did, it was another six months before she agreed to sleep with him. She thought he would give up his pursuit, but he kept coming back. After eighteen months Renee believed he was truly serious about wanting a future together. She hadn't known that during a wild, uninhibited week in Vegas he'd married a long-legged dancer.

"What are you doing here?" Her query came out in a breathless whisper.

"I live here."

Renee felt heat sweep over her face and neck. "I know you live here, Sheldon, but I didn't expect you to be sitting on the steps." Light from hallway sconces did not permit her to see his expression.

"I was waiting to talk to you." He patted his knees. "Please sit down."

She shook her head. "I can't. I need to change for dinner." His right hand snaked out, caught her wrist and pulled her down onto his lap. Renee squirmed, but she couldn't free herself. "Please let me go."

He buried his hair in her hair. "Indulge me, Renee. Just for a few minutes."

Relaxing in his embrace, Renee luxuriated in the muscled thighs under her hips and the unyielding strength in the arms holding her in a protective embrace. Oh, she'd missed those arms around her; she'd missed Sheldon.

"What do you want to talk about?"

"About what happened two weeks ago."

She stiffened before relaxing again. "What about it?"

Sheldon pressed a kiss to her fragrant hair. "I want to apologize if you feel I was not supportive of you."

"All I asked of you was to be a friend, to support me during the good and bad times, but I got a lover instead."

"I am your friend, darling—friend, lover *and* protector. I wanted to tell you to forget about Susanna and Valerie, but you were too upset for me to reason with you. They said what they said because they're jealous."

"They can't be jealous of me, Sheldon."

He pressed a kiss along the column of her neck. "They are, sweetheart. We have no control over what another person says or thinks, but if any of what they said about you in that bathroom gets back to me, then there's going to be hell to pay."

Covering the hands cradling her belly, Renee shook her head. "I didn't tell you so that you could fight with someone. I just wanted to let you know why I don't want to attend any more soirees with you."

"You don't have..." Whatever he intended to say died on Sheldon's lips when he felt movement under his hand. His expression changed, features softening. "When did she start kicking you?"

Renee smiled at Sheldon over her shoulder. "Last week. At first they were flutters, but they're much stronger now."

"She's a frisky little thing," he said with a broad smile.

"She sleeps all day, then wakes up and performs somersaults half the night."

"Does she keep you up?"

"Sometimes." Renee eased Sheldon's hands away from her belly. "I have to go get ready for dinner." She moved off his lap; he also rose to his feet.

"I'll wait downstairs for you."

"I'm not eating at the dining hall."

"You're going out?"

"Yes."

"Off the farm?"

"Why?"

Sheldon crossed his arms over his chest, deciding on honesty. "Jeremy told me about your telephone call."

"He had no right to tell you about a personal conversation."

"If it was so personal, then you could've either called your party back or asked Jeremy to leave the room."

Renee rolled her eyes at Sheldon. "One does not ask one's boss to leave the room to indulge in a personal telephone conversation during work hours. Besides, he shouldn't have told you my business."

"Jeremy told me because as long as you live and work here you *are* his business. You, thirty-five others, thirty-six including the child you're carrying, and half a billion dollars in horseflesh. Don't ever forget that, Renee.

"If you leave the farm, then you will be accompanied either by me or an armed escort. Security has already been tightened around the property. Now, I'm going to ask you again, Renee. Are you leaving the farm tonight?" He had enunciated each word.

There was a long, brittle silence as Renee struggled to keep her raw emotions in check. After ending the call with her brother she'd forced herself not to think about Donald. If he had divorced his wife in order to propose marriage, did he actually believe she would marry him now?

No. She could not and would not even if she were carrying quintuplets. Not when she had fallen in love with another man, a man who had become her friend, lover and protector.

"No, Sheldon. I'm not leaving the farm tonight."

Moving closer, he cradled her face and brushed a kiss at the corners of her mouth. "Shall I wait up for you?"

Renee wanted to tell Sheldon he was being controlling, but offered him a saucy smile instead. There was no doubt he wanted to make certain she was safe.

"Only if you wish. Perhaps when I return we can have a sleepover."

Throwing back his head, Sheldon laughed, the sound rich and full-throated. "I'm looking forward to it, princess."

Rising on tiptoe, she kissed his clean-shaven cheek, then made her way down the hallway to her bedroom. She had been invited to share dinner with Kelly, Tricia and Beatrice Miller, followed by a game of bidwhist.

Renee rang the doorbell to Kelly and Ryan's home, pushed open the door and walked into bright light, heat and mouthwatering smells.

Tricia appeared from the rear of the house, a bright smile softening her round face. "Hi. Come on back to the kitchen."

Renee noticed Tricia's curly hair was longer than when she'd been introduced to her. Thick black shiny curls fell over her ears and the nape of her neck. Tricia Blackstone was blooming—all over.

She walked into the kitchen and into a flurry of activity. Beatrice Miller stood at the cooking island slicing an avocado, while Kelly browned chicken cutlets in a frying pan. Kelly's daughter, four-month-old Vivienne, sat in a high chair, patting the chair's table as Tricia resumed spooning food into her bird-like mouth.

Beatrice, a petite woman with salt-and-pepper hair and smooth dark brown skin had a slender body that rivaled women half her age. A quick smile, soft drawling voice and a gentle manner made her the perfect companion for Gus Parker.

The four women, ranging in age from sixty to mid-thirties, shared a warm smile. "Thank you for coming," Kelly said.

Renee nodded. "Thank you for inviting me. Can I help with something?"

Kelly shook her head. "Not this time. The first time you're a guest. The next time you can do something more strenuous like set the table."

Renee could not stop the rush of heat flooding her face. "I'm pregnant, not physically challenged."

"Not yet," chorused Kelly and Tricia.

Kelly stared at Renee's belly. "By the time you're ready to deliver you won't be able to bend over to tie your own shoes."

"Stop teasing the child," Beatrice chided softly. "She's carrying rather nicely."

"When are you due, Renee?" Tricia asked.

"March third."

Tricia sucked her teeth. "I'm due the beginning of July and already I can't fit into my slacks."

Kelly stared at her sister-in-law. "I told you even before you knew you were pregnant that I dreamt you were holding three fish. And that means you're going to have triplets."

Tricia sucked her teeth again, this time rolling her eyes at Kelly. "You and your lying dreams."

Beatrice nodded. "You know the old folks say when you dream of fish you're going to hear of a pregnancy."

"I know for certain I'm having one," Renee said quietly.

"Girl or boy?" Beatrice asked as she sliced a ripe mango.

"Girl."

Kelly pressed her hands together. "Wonderful. Now Vivienne will have someone close to her age to play with."

"May I feed her?" The question was out before Renee could censor herself.

Tricia looked at Renee and smiled. "Sure."

"Where can I wash my hands?"

Tricia pointed to a door at the opposite end of the kitchen. "A bathroom is over there."

The three women exchanged knowing glances as Renee went into the bathroom. "She's going to need the practice before you, Tricia," Kelly whispered to her sister-in-law.

Renee returned, exchanging seats with Tricia. Vivienne Blackstone was a beautiful little girl. She'd inherited her mother's looks and her father's curly black hair; her eye color had compromised. It was gunmetal-gray.

Over a dinner of chicken piccata, linguine with roasted garlic and oil, a tropical salad of smoked chicken with avocados and mangoes, toasted Italian bread and lemon sorbet, followed by a lively card game, Kelly and Tricia became the girlfriends Renee had left behind in Miami. Beatrice provided the sage advice she occasionally sought from her mother.

Ryan and Sean had returned from the dining hall in time to put Vivienne to bed; they retreated to the family room to watch a movie, leaving the women to their card game.

"Where did you learn to play bidwhist?" Kelly asked Renee.

"I used to watch my mother and aunts. How did you learn?"

Kelly smiled. "From my mother. She and her sorority sisters used to get together and play Sunday afternoons when they were in college."

"How about you?" Renee asked Tricia.

"My grandmother taught me."

Beatrice stared across the table at Renee. "Do young people still play?"

"I don't think so. Some of the college students who worked part-time at the law firm where I worked talked about playing spades."

Tricia laid down a card. "That's too bad. I suppose we're going to have to keep the tradition going."

"You're right," Kelly concurred. "If Sheldon and his wild bunch can hang out at his cabin to play poker, smoke cigars and drink beer for their annual fall camping weekend, then I suggest we get together every other month for a bidwhist party."

Tricia stared at her grandfather's fiancée. "Did you smell cigar smoke on my grandfather when he got back this afternoon?"

Beatrice shook her head. "No. Gus swore he

didn't take one puff and neither did Sheldon, who told the other two guys that they couldn't smoke inside the cabin."

"They need to give up the cigars *and* the beer. It takes them two days to empty a keg," Tricia grumbled.

"Get out!" Renee gasped. "That's a lot of beer."

Kelly put down her cards and placed a hand on her hip. "Why don't you talk to your man?"

Renee's eyes widened. "Sheldon's not my man!"

Kelly lifted an eyebrow. "I didn't mention Sheldon's name. Gotcha!" she teased, pointing a finger at Renee.

Tricia peered over the top of her cards. "Is my father-in-law your man-n-n-n, Renee?" she drawled singsong.

"I'm not telling," Renee teased back, flashing a dimpled grin.

Leaning across the table, Kelly and Tricia exchanged high-five handshakes. "Boo-yaw!" they chorused in unison.

Renee laughed until her sides hurt.

She was still chuckling under her breath as she climbed the porch steps and found Sheldon sitting on a rocker waiting for her. He rose to his feet, extended his arms and she moved into his embrace.

Burying her face in the soft fibers of his sweater, Renee felt safe, safer than she had ever been in her life. Even safer than when she'd slept in the Miami

Beach mansion surrounded by gates, guard dogs and high-tech electronic surveillance equipment.

Easing back, she smiled up at Sheldon. "Are you ready for our sleepover?"

He returned her smile. "Yes, I am."

Renee did not have time to catch her breath as he lifted her off her feet and carried her into the house. Sheldon shifted her body, locked the door and then headed for the staircase.

Sheldon did not walk to the end of hallway, but stopped before they reached his bedroom, lifting a questioning eyebrow. Every time he and Renee made love he had come to her. The only exception had been their first encounter at the cabin. However, the day of reckoning could not be postponed forever. He had to know whether she wanted him in her life as much as he wanted her.

"Yours or mine?"

Renee did not know how, but she knew what Sheldon was feeling at that moment. The doubts, questions as to where they and their relationship were heading, and if what they shared went beyond sharing a bed and their passion.

Closing her eyes, she affected a secret smile. "Yours."

Sheldon lowered his head and pressed a kiss to the top of her head. In that instant all that made Renee Wilson who she was seeped into him, becoming a part of him.

It had taken three days away from her, three days where he and three of his best friends had gotten together for their annual fall camping weekend, to remind him what had been missing in his life.

The wild bunch, as they'd called themselves, had become longtime friends who left the farm to kick back for several days of male bonding. They fished, hunted, cooked, smoked cigars, drank beer, swapped war stories and talked about the women they'd loved and lost. These men had become the brothers Sheldon always wanted, but never had. They were his confidants and his conscience.

However, this year it was different, different because although he had brought women to the cabin, none of them had touched the part of him that ached for more than a physical release. None of them were able to make him look beyond the basic human need of food, shelter and clothes for the one thing every human being needed for ultimate survival and perpetuation of oneself: love.

He'd stopped trying to rationalize why Renee had come to him carrying another man's child beneath her heart. Why her and not some other woman, unencumbered by her past. And why did he feel so completely helpless whenever he thought about what she needed most: a husband. Jeremy's parting cryptic statement was imprinted on his brain: "look at what you have, and what you could hope to have."

He had enough money to last him well into old age, had transferred a horse-racing legacy to the next generation and had set aside ten thousand acres of prime property for his grandchildren. He had everything a man could ever hope for—everything but a woman to share his future and the dreams he had for the second half of his life. Every time he opened his mouth to say the two most blissful words a woman yearned to hear, they died on his lips.

He remembered his mother on her deathbed begging his father to "marry" her before she drew her last painful breath. And, although James Blackstone knew he was breaking the law and could have been sent to jail, he had married the woman whom he had loved.

Let go of the fear, his inner voice whispered. Renee wasn't Julia and he was no longer a thirty-two-year-old single father with two young sons who depended on him for their daily needs. *Marry her,* the voice continued. And if he did marry, Renee and her daughter would become Virginia Blackstones, a name with clout and influence.

Walking into the bedroom, he placed her on the king-size bed. The side of the mattress dipped with his weight as he sat beside Renee. A loud pop, followed by a brilliant shower of burning embers behind a decorative fireplace screen threw macabre shadows on the whitewashed ceiling and walls.

Leaning over, Sheldon quietly, seductively removed and then placed Renee's clothing on the bench at the foot of the large bed.

Renee did not open her eyes as she luxuriated in the gossamer touch of Sheldon's fingertips as he sculpted the roundness of her swollen belly before moving up to trace the outline of her engorged breasts. One hand slipped between her knees, moving upward and parting her thighs as it traveled toward the source of heat and the soft throbbing making it almost impossible for her to lie motionless.

Reaching for his hand, she held it against her moist, pulsing warmth, unable to stop the moans coming from her constricted throat. If Sheldon did not take her—quickly—it would be over within seconds. His finger searched and found her. It was his turn to groan when her flesh convulsed around his digit.

Pulling back, he sat on his heels and pulled the sweater over his head. Within seconds his slacks and underwear were pooled on the floor. Gently, he shifted Renee until her buttocks were pressed to his groin. He rested her top leg over his, then eased his swollen flesh into her, both moaning in satisfaction as their bodies melded as one.

I'm home, the scalding blood in Renee's veins sang. It wasn't the modest house where she'd grown up in a Miami suburb; it wasn't the shabby apartment where she'd lived with her mother and brother after her father's untimely death; it wasn't the small condominium apartment she'd bought after working two jobs to save enough money for the down payment; and it certainly wasn't the palatial beachfront mansion with views of the Atlantic Ocean and passing luxury yachts and cruise ships in the distance. Sheldon Blackstone was home and everything the word represented: love, safety, comfort and protection.

Closing her eyes, she tried concentrating on anything but the hardness sliding in and out of her body. Her heart rate skyrocketed along with the uneven rhythm of her breathing. She experienced extreme heat, then bone-chilling cold that made her teeth chatter. Sheldon had set a pace that quickened, slowed, then quickened again until she was mindless with an ecstasy that had become a mind-altering trip shattering her into millions of pieces before lulling her back to a euphoric state that left her weak and mewling as a newborn.

Sheldon clenched his teeth as he fought a hopeless battle. He did not want to let go—release the passion streaking along the edges of sanity. He wanted the whirling, swirling sensations to last—forever if possible. The passion Renee wrung from him hurtled him to heights of erotic pleasure he had never experienced before—not with any woman. He quickened his movements, mindful of the child kicking vigorously in her womb, then went completely still as he moaned and poured out his passions in a flood tide that made him forget everything.

They lay joined, waiting until their hearts resumed

a normal rate. Sheldon moved once to pull the sheet and blanket up and over their moist bodies, then as one they fell into a deep sated sleep.

Ten

Renee slipped out of Sheldon's bed early Thanksgiving morning, retreating to her old bedroom to shower. She hadn't slept there since the night of her bidwhist party with Kelly, Tricia and Beatrice.

Her daily routine had changed since she'd begun sleeping in Sheldon's bedroom. She retired earlier and woke up earlier. Weather permitting she usually took a morning walk. And what Sheldon had told her about additional security around the perimeter of the farm had become apparent whenever she spied a man sitting on horseback with a rifle resting in the crook of an arm or slung across his chest.

Dressed in a bulky sweater, stretch pants, boots

and a baseball cap, she set out on her walk. A haze hung over the valley like a diaphanous blue-gray veil. Although a national holiday it was not a farm holiday. Horses had to be washed, groomed and turned out into the paddocks for daily exercise.

Her early morning walks were now a part of her daily exercise regimen. The added weight had put pressure on her lower back, but since she'd begun walking it eased.

Forty minutes and a mile later, she stood in front of one of four barns where the thoroughbreds were stabled. Several grooms were hosing down horses. She spied Shah Jahan as he stood motionless under the stream of water sluicing over his ebony coat. She couldn't pull her gaze away from the long arching neck, noble head and the sleek powerful lines in half a ton of regal horseflesh. Jahan had raced twice since the International Gold Cup, and had come in first both times. The scorecard with Jahan's racing statistics read:

Owner: Blackstone Farms
Trainer: Kevin Manning
Sire: Ali Jahir Dam: Jane's Way
Starts: 3 Wins: 3 Earnings: $1.2 million

What had most people in the world of thoroughbred racing wagging their heads was the fact that Shah Jahan had yet to celebrate his second birthday.

Nodding to the grooms, Renee walked into the barn. The sounds of stalls being swept out reverberated in the large space. The sweet smell of hay masked the odor of sweat, manure and urine.

She stepped aside just in time to avoid a ball of black and white fur scampering around her feet. Leaning down, she picked up a tiny puppy. It wiggled and yelped as it struggled to free itself.

"To whom do you belong?"

"No one, Miss Renee."

Turning on her heel, Renee stared at Peter McCann, a teenager whose pleasant looks were neutralized by an outbreak of acne.

"Is he a stray?" she asked.

Peter nodded. "His mama whelped a litter about six weeks ago. Dr. Blackstone has already given away four. He's the only one left. Doc already gave him his shots."

Renee smiled at the large black eyes staring back at her. "What breed is he?"

"Mutt," Peter replied, deadpan. "His mama is part lab and sheepdog. Don't know about his papa. Lady Day must have snuck off the farm when she was in heat and found herself a man. She didn't come back until she was ready to whelp. Now that she's weaned this last one Dr. Blackstone plans to neuter her. He claims we have enough dogs to keep the horses company."

Sheldon had explained to Renee that most horse farms kept either dogs or goats as pets to keep the stabled horses, which are by nature social animals, company. She did not know why, but she felt an instant kinship with the puppy.

"I think I'm going to take him home with me."

"He's going to be a big one, Miss Renee. Take a look at his paws."

She looked at his paws. They were rather large for a small puppy. "If he's part sheepdog, then he'll adapt to staying outdoors."

"None of the farm dogs come inside, except when it snows. If you're going to take him home, then I'll get a leash for you. I'll also bring over some food after I finish up with my chores."

Renee gave him a warm smile. "Thank you."

It wasn't until after she had attached the leash to the collar around the puppy's neck that she thought about Sheldon. Would he even want a dog in his house? Had his sons grown up with pets?

She hadn't had a pet of her own since her mother was forced to sell their house and move into an apartment where the landlord had posted a sign prohibiting pets of any kind.

The puppy tired, stopped and sat down. Squatting, she picked up the dog, cradling it against her jacket. She'd just walked past Jeremy and Tricia's house when she saw Sheldon striding toward her. A sensual smile curved her mouth. He had a sexy walk. His back ramrod-straight, he swaggered, broad shoulders swaying from side to side.

Slowing her pace, she smiled, stopped and waited for him to approach her. He'd elected to wear a flannel shirt with jeans and a pair of worn boots.

She'd seen him dressed in a tailored suit, a tuxedo and jeans with a pullover sweater or cotton shirt, and she liked him dressed down best. The casual attire seemed to enhance his rugged handsomeness.

Her smile faded the moment she noticed his stern-faced expression. "Good morning."

Sheldon's gray eyes swept over Renee, lingering momentarily on the puppy cradled against her chest. "I thought because it wasn't a work day you'd stay in bed beyond daybreak."

"I enjoy getting up early and walking."

"Why don't you wait for me to walk with you." His tone was softer, almost conciliatory.

"I don't want to wake you up."

"Wake me up, Renee."

"Okay, Sheldon. I'll wake you up."

He pointed to the puppy. "What do you have there?"

"A pet."

He lifted both eyebrows. "A pet?"

"Our pet, Sheldon."

He crossed his arms over his chest. "Did I say I wanted or needed a pet?"

Renee shook her head. "No. But, if I'm going to live with you then he will become *our* pet." She peered up at him. "Don't you like animals?"

Sheldon gave Renee an incredulous look. "If I

didn't like animals why would I own a horse farm? I'm not opposed to you having a dog, but who's going to take care of him when we go away?"

"When are we going away?"

"I'd planned to take you to the cabin this weekend. You said you wanted to learn how to fish."

"Can't we take him with us, Sheldon? Please," she added when a frown appeared between his eyes.

The corners of his mouth twitched then inched upward as he tried and failed to bite back a grin. "Yes, princess. You can bring *our* pet to the cabin."

Moving closer, she wound her free arm around his waist, encountering a bulge in the small of his back. "Sheldon." His name was a weak whisper. He was carrying a handgun.

Grasping her hand, he pulled it away from his body. "It's all right, baby."

"It's not all right. I don't like guns."

"Neither do I," he countered. "But sometimes they are a necessary evil."

She took a step backward. "I don't want to see it."

"Walk ahead of me and you won't see it."

Renee moved in front of Sheldon. She could feel his gaze boring into her back. "I need a name for the puppy."

"Is it a boy?" She nodded. "How about Patch?"

"How did you come up with that one?"

"Because he looks as if he's wearing a black patch over one eye."

Renee stared at the sleeping puppy. So much for her being observant.

"Patch Blackstone. I like the sound of that," she said, peering at Sheldon over her shoulder.

"He's going to need food."

"Peter promised to bring some to the house."

Sheldon shook his head. Three months ago he lived alone. Now he had not only a woman but also a dog sharing his home. "Try to paper train him as soon as possible, because I don't want more work for Claire."

"I'll clean up after him."

"No, you won't."

"Why not, Sheldon? He's my pet and therefore my responsibility."

"You don't need to be on your knees cleaning up dog crap. I'll do it."

Renee's back stiffened. "No, you won't."

"If that's the case, then get rid of the damn dog." She stopped, spun around and walked back to face him. "I'm not going to argue with you, Renee," he warned in a deceptively soft voice.

There was something about Sheldon's expression that stilled Renee's tongue. His implacable expression was unnerving. "Nor I you," she said quietly.

Turning on her heel, she bit down on her lower lip until it pulsed between her teeth. How could she prove her point with a man who refused to debate?

The answer was she couldn't.

* * *

Renee sat next to Sheldon at a table in the dining hall. Each table's centerpiece was representative of the season: tiny pumpkins, gourds, sprigs of pine and pine cones. Orange and yellow tablecloths had replaced the usual white. Prerecorded taped music provided a nice backdrop for the various conversations from the diners.

She'd had a light breakfast because she wanted to save her appetite for Thanksgiving dinner. Within minutes Kevin Manning, his wife and their niece, Cheryl, joined them.

Nineteen-year-old Cheryl had become a racing celebrity. Barely five feet in height, she topped the scales at an even one hundred pounds.

Ryan Blackstone stood up, waiting for conversations to fade. He smiled, flashing sparkling white teeth under a neatly barbered mustache. "Good afternoon. Unlike my esteemed father and brother, I'll make this speech short and sweet, because I don't know about you but I'm hungry enough to eat a horse."

There came a round of hisses and boos when he mentioned horse. "Not any of our horses, of course." This was followed with applause. Ryan sobered. "But on a more serious note, I'd like to give thanks for so many things this year. I'm thankful for our families, immediate and extended. We also have to thank Kevin and Cheryl for their incredible successes. We are thankful and grateful for the new members of our farm family." He smiled at Renee and Beatrice.

"I'd also like to thank my brother for his hard work and unwavering support as we prepare for another generation of Blackstone Farms achievements. I'd like to thank my father for always being here not only for me but also for all of us. He's sacrificed a lot to make Blackstone Farms what it is today, and for that I'm certain he will be rewarded in ways he cannot imagine.

"Last year our mothers came to Sheldon because they wanted a safe environment for their children. That request gave birth to the Blackstone Farm Day School and Infant Center. This year some of you have asked for a place of worship, and your request has been taken under advisement. Sheldon has offered to give up five acres of land in the north end for the construction of an interdenominational church. The contractor laid the foundation two days ago, and we hope to have the project completed before spring."

Ryan paused as applause and whistles rent the air. He held up a hand. "Some of you may not be aware of it, but in another life one of our grooms served as an assistant pastor in a little church in Texas." He motioned to a table to his right. "Reverend Jimmy Merrell, I'd like for you to meet your flock and bless the food." There were gasps of surprise intermingled with applause.

Jimmy stood up and clasped his hands, everyone following suit. Renee folded her hands in her lap. She gave Sheldon a sidelong glance when his hand covered hers.

There were so many things to be thankful for this year: the child kicking vigorously inside her; the love of the man cradling her hand; the love and happiness her mother had found after so many years of pain and despair, and her brother for his love and support after she'd come to him when she needed him most.

The invocation concluded and the feasting began. Renee ate so much that she had to refuse dessert. She'd wanted to sample the pastry chef's renowned sweet potato pie, and in the end she had a slice wrapped up to take with her before she and Sheldon left for their weekend at the cabin.

Sheldon cradled Renee to his chest, staring into the flickering flames in the fireplace. A gentle smile touched his mouth. It was a perfect scenario: a man and woman in bed together while their dog slept on a rug in front of the fireplace.

He'd come to the cabin with Renee because he needed to be away from the farm…and alone with her. Here he hoped he would be able to face his fear and come to terms with his feelings for her. He had known there was something special about her from the very beginning, yet he could not have imagined he would fall in love with a woman carrying the fruit of her love for another man inside her.

Once he'd recovered from the shock that she was pregnant it had become insignificant. Kelly had married Ryan and had become mother to Sean, his son from a prior marriage. Kelly had legally adopted Sean the year before.

Sheldon closed his eyes, sighing softly. If he married Renee before the birth of her daughter, then she would automatically become a Blackstone.

"Have you thought of a name for the baby?"

Renee snuggled closer and wiggled her nose when the hair on Sheldon's chest tickled her. "I've thought of a few."

"Do you want to tell me, or it is a secret?"

"It's not a secret. I'm considering Virginia, because it was my grandmother's name. I also like Sonya and Hannah."

"They're all strong, traditional feminine names. Have you picked out ones for a boy, just in case?"

Pulling out of his embrace, Renee sat up. "I can't have a boy."

Sheldon noted the look of distress on her face. "Why not? Sonograms aren't always that accurate."

Tunneling her fingers through her hair, Renee held it off her face. "I don't want a boy, because..." Her words trailed off, locked in her throat.

Reaching for her, Sheldon pulled her up to sit on his lap. "Why not, Renee?"

She stared at him in the wavering light from the fireplace fire. "A boy needs a mother *and* a father. I know I can raise my daughter by myself, but not my son."

"I'll help you, darling."

She froze. "What?"

"I'll help you raise your son. I've made mistakes with Ryan and Jeremy, yet they've turned out all right. I'm very proud of them."

Renee shook her head. "No, Sheldon. I can't ask you to do that."

"Didn't you ask me to protect you and your baby?"

"Protect, not assume responsibility for raising it."

A weighted heaviness settled in Sheldon's chest as he digested Renee's statement. She would permit him in her life but not to share in it.

His life had come full circle. Julia had married him, borne his two sons, yet she had withheld a part of herself from him, had concealed her illness until it was too late.

Was he destined to repeat the same mistake? Had he fallen in love with a woman like Julia?

Now it was his turn to hide, hide his true feelings from Renee. He had fallen in love with her, would probably always love her, but it was something he would never reveal to her or anyone else.

He squeezed her shoulder. "Let's get some sleep because we're going to have get up early tomorrow to go fishing."

* * *

"Let's go, sleepyhead. Time to get up." Renee mumbled in her sleep, but did not wake up. Sheldon shook her harder. "Renee."

Her lids fluttered wildly as she opened her eyes. Where was she? She heard a soft yelping and came awake. Rolling over on her back she saw Sheldon leaning over her.

"What time is it?"

"Four," he whispered.

"Four o'clock in the freaking morning?"

Grinning, he nodded. "Let's go while the fish are biting." He nuzzled her ear. "Okay, princess. If I catch the fish you'll have to clean them."

Renee sat straight up. She hated cleaning fish. "No. Give me a few minutes and I'll be ready."

Sheldon sat down on the side of the bed, watching her as she walked to the bathroom. She was moving more slowly now. Cupping a hand over his mouth, he closed his eyes.

He had spent a restless night wondering whether he'd coerced Renee into living with him. Renovations on her bungalow were nearing completion, and he thought about giving her the option of moving out of his house and into her own.

But seeing her waddle across the room while massaging her lower back squeezed his heart. He couldn't leave her—not now. Not until after she delivered the baby.

* * *

Renee lay on a wooden bench in the bathroom, her legs covered with foam. Sheldon straddled the bench, razor in hand. He had offered to shave her legs.

He raised her foot to his thigh. "Relax, baby. I'm not going to cut you."

"I've always shaved my own legs."

Leaning forward, he laid a hand over her distended belly. "That was before, when you could bend down or lift your leg. Right now, you're at my mercy."

Staring up at the recessed lights, Renee nodded. "That's what I'm afraid of."

His right hand moved up her thighs and covered the furred mound. "You know I wouldn't take advantage of you."

She slapped at his hand. "I know nothing of the sort."

"Maybe if I shave a little higher the hospital won't charge you for that particular procedure once you go into labor."

"Stop it, Sheldon!" She laughed so hard that her stomach muscles contracted. "Now, I'm hurting," she said between guffaws.

"Where?"

"My sides and back."

Hovering over her, Sheldon smiled. "I'll give you a massage after I finish your legs."

Renee calmed down enough to remain still as he drew the blade over her legs.

Sheldon finished one leg, then did the other. Gathering her off the bench, he cradled her to his chest.

"I think you've gained a few pounds since yesterday."

Renee met his gaze. "Did you see how much I ate for Thanksgiving?"

He shook his head. "No, because I was too busy stuffing my own face."

"I hope the doctor won't put me on a diet after I weigh in."

"How much have you gained overall?"

"Twelve pounds." She'd doubled her weight gain since coming to the farm.

"That's not much."

"I know. But there are times when I feel like a beached whale."

"You look beautiful."

Tightening her hold on his neck, Renee kissed his stubbly jaw. "You're so good for a woman's ego."

He angled his head. "You are beautiful, Renee."

"Thank you. I'd like to cook for you tonight, Sheldon."

"Are you sure you know how to cook?"

She remembered another time when he'd doubted her culinary skills. "Stay out of the kitchen, and you'll see if I can. I'm going to check your refrigerator and freezer, and if you don't have what I need then you're going to have to drive me to the nearest supermarket."

He placed her on her side on a table in a steam room. "There are no supermarkets around here."

"Where do you buy your food?"

"I usually bring it from the farm."

"Like the keg of beer you and your buddies drink during your annual fall frolic."

"If I tell you something, will you promise not to tell anyone?"

Sheldon's expression was so serious Renee felt her heart stop before starting up again. "Yes."

"We usually drink a couple of six-packs, not a keg."

"Tricia said her grandfather brags about you guys emptying a keg in a couple of days."

Pulling over a stool, Sheldon sat down and gently kneaded the muscles in Renee's lower back. "The first year we got together we bought a keg. We emptied the keg by pouring out more than three quarters of the beer. I'm lucky if I can drink two beers in one sitting."

"Then it's all a lie?"

He pressed his mouth to her bare shoulder. "It wasn't a lie. When I said we emptied a keg everyone assumed we had actually drunk a keg of beer. We never bothered to clarify the misconception because that would destroy the wild bunch's mystique. Do you know how many guys want in our elite organization?"

Renee laughed again. "You guys are a fraud."

"And you better not tell," Sheldon threatened.

"I'll think about it."

"Renee!"

"Okay, Sheldon. I'll keep your secret."

Rounding the table, he hunkered down and kissed her until her lips parted to his probing tongue. The kiss claimed a dreamy intimacy that hinted of more as Sheldon gathered Renee off the table and carried her into one of the downstairs bedrooms. He lowered her to the bed, his body following; he supported his weight on his elbows.

Reversing their positions, Sheldon pressed his back to the headboard and brought Renee to straddle him, her back against his chest. Lifting her slightly, he entered her, covering her breasts with his hands. The coupling lasted minutes, but when they climaxed simultaneously it was to offer the other the sweetest ecstasy either had ever experienced.

Eleven

Renee stood at the cooking island, adding chopped fresh rosemary to a lemon marinade for the trout she'd planned to cook on the stovetop grill.

"Do you need me for anything before I go upstairs and wash my hair?" Sheldon asked as he walked into the kitchen. He had taken Sean with him to Staunton for a haircut.

She smiled at Sheldon. "No. I'm good here."

After sharing cooking duties over the Thanksgiving weekend, she and Sheldon continued the ritual once they returned to the farm. He had been so impressed with her cooking skills that he had begun making special requests.

He left the bed when she did, accompanying her on early morning walks, and returning to the house after stopping for breakfast at the dining hall. She had adjusted her work hours from nine-to-five to eight-to-four. Although she no longer required a nap during the day, she rarely slept soundly through the night. As soon as she got into bed the baby began her nightly aerobic workout.

She concentrated on whisking the marinade, then placed it on a shelf in the refrigerator. Removing a platter with two cleaned and filleted trout, she lightly salted them, added freshly ground pepper, wrapped two slices of bacon around each fish and tucked bay leaves inside the fold close to the skin of the fish.

Sheldon entered the kitchen as Renee was putting the finishing touches on the meal.

Renee took several steps, stopping inches from the man whom she had fallen in love with and rested her head over his heart. It was pounding a runaway rhythm. "Talk to me, Sheldon."

Reaching out and pulling her to his body, he rocked her gently. "I love you, Renee. I love you, yet I'm afraid of losing you."

Tilting her chin, she saw pain in his eyes before he shuttered his gaze. "Why on earth would you lose me?" she whispered. "I plan to be around for a long time."

He released her shoulders, cradling her face between his hands. "I want you in my life not for a few months or for a few years, but for always. I know I can be a good father to your baby, but I doubt whether I can be a good husband to you."

"Why, Sheldon?"

Lowering his head, he pressed his mouth to her ear, telling Renee about Julia, her illness and his selfish pursuit to make horse-racing history.

"I saw her grow weaker and weaker, but whenever I asked if she was all right she reassured me she was okay. And like a fool I believed her."

"It's not as if you didn't ask her, darling. She just chose not to tell you the truth."

"I should've insisted."

Renee shook her head. "That wouldn't have changed a thing. Not when you live with someone who chooses to conceal the truth."

Sheldon pulled himself from his past and back to the present. *Not when you live with someone who chooses to conceal the truth.*

Julia had deceived him, and Donald had deceived Renee. The difference was Julia was gone and Renee was here. He should ask her to marry him and claim her child as his own.

But could he risk it?

"Yes," he said softly.

Renee stared at Sheldon. "Yes, what?"

He blinked as if coming out of a trance. "Do you love me, Renee?"

A flicker of apprehension coursed through her.

Was Sheldon losing his mind? "What's going on with you?"

"Do you love me, Renee Wilson?" He'd enunciated each word as if she were hard of hearing.

Her lids fluttered wildly, keeping time with her runaway pulse. "Yes, I do, Sheldon Blackstone. I do love you."

"Will you do me the honor of becoming my wife?" She hesitated. "Yes or no, Renee?"

"Yes."

"And will you also permit me the honor to be a father to your daughter?"

As their gazes met, Renee felt a shock run through her. Sheldon was offering her what she had wanted all of her life: a man she could love *and* trust, a man who would protect her *and* her baby.

She bit down on her lower lip to still its trembling. "Yes, Sheldon." A delicious shudder heated her body when he dipped his head and kissed her. "Will this arrangement be strictly business?" she whispered against his mouth.

Lines fanned out around his incredible eyes. "Oh, it will be business, all right. I want to marry you before the end of year, turn one of the upstairs bedrooms into a nursery, then when Virginia, Sonya or Hannah Blackstone is at least six months old we're going to go on a belated honeymoon to somewhere exotic and make mad, passionate love to each other."

Giggling and snuggling as close as her belly would allow her, Renee curved her arms under his shoulders. “We don’t have to go away to make mad, passionate love to each other.”

Sheldon placed a hand over her middle. “Just once I’d like to make love to you without our daughter coming between us.”

“Three months, then another six weeks. It’s not that far off.”

“You’re right. I think I’m going to like having a daughter.”

“I’m sure she’s going to love having you for her father.”

His hands moving up and down her back in a soothing motion, Sheldon rested his chin on the top of Renee’s head. “I’m going to tell you now that I’m going to spoil her, Renee.”

“That’s okay as long as she doesn’t become a brat.”

“Let’s have dinner, then we’ll call Jeremy and Ryan and let them in on our good news. After that we’ll call your folks.”

“I think I’d like to have a Christmas Eve wedding.”

“And you will, princess. You can have any and everything you want.”

Renee knew there was something special about Sheldon Blackstone the instant she stepped out of her car to find him staring down at her. So special that she fell in love with him despite her vow never to trust another man.

Christmas Eve

White damask tablecloths, delicate china, crystal stemware, sterling silver, beeswax tapers in sterling holders and large pine wreaths decorated with white satin bows and white rosebuds at Blackstone Farms' dining hall set the stage for the nuptials between Renee Anna Wilson and Sheldon James Blackstone.

Rumors were circulating throughout Virginia's horse country that there was to be a wedding at Blackstone Farms, and for the first time in farm history no one deigned to confirm or deny the rumor.

Sheldon had selected Jeremy as his best man, Ryan and Sean as his groomsmen. Renee had asked her brother to give her away, her sister-in-law had agreed to be her maid-of-honor and Kelly and Tricia were her bridesmaids.

The farms' employees began filing into the dining hall at seven forty-five, sitting at assigned tables. A string quartet played Mozart concertos, then at exactly eight o'clock, the lights dimmed. Jeremy and Sheldon, dressed in formalwear, entered the dining hall. An eerie hush fell over the room as groomsmen with burgundy silk ties and bridesmaids in floor-length matching gowns followed the procession.

The distinctive strains of the wedding march began and Renee, clinging to her brother's arm, concentrated on putting one foot in front of the other as she made her way over the white carpet leading to where Sheldon waited in front of the stained-glass window. Her dress, an off-white, long-sleeved satin gown with an empire waist, was designed to artfully camouflage her swollen belly. She looked at her mother and smiled.

Edward Wilson tightened his hold on his sister's hand. "We're almost there, Rennie."

Edward had contacted Donald Rush after Renee informed him that she was marrying Sheldon, and told him that his sister had married. Donald offered his best wishes for her happiness, then abruptly hung up. The telephone call had closed the door on Renee and Donald's past.

Renee let out a soft gasp as she felt a strong kick. Her baby had awakened in time to celebrate her parents' wedding. She focused her attention on the Reverend Jimmy Merrell, who waited to perform his first wedding as the farm's resident minister.

After midnight, when Renee lay in the warmth of her husband's embrace, she recalled her wedding and the reception dinner that followed. The resident chefs had outdone themselves with a reception that included passed hors d'oeuvres, seafood, carving and Asian stations. A seated dinner menu offered soup, salad, blue lump crab cakes and entrées of rib-eye steak and free-range chicken breast.

Shifting to her right side, she placed her left hand

over her husband's chest, the light from a table lamp glinting off the precious stones in her wedding band.

Sheldon squeezed the tiny hand, whispering a silent prayer of thanksgiving for his wife and the child kicking in her womb. He had been given a second chance to be a good husband. This time he was certain he would get it right.

"Do you want to know something, Sheldon?"

"What, darling?"

"I just realized how lucky I am."

"Why?"

"I get to have a sleepover with my best friend every single night."

Chuckling softly, Sheldon kissed her forehead. "Merry Christmas, princess."

Renee kissed his shoulder. "Merry Christmas, my love."

This Christmas they would celebrate as husband and wife.

The next one would be as husband, wife, mother and father.

Epilogue

Eighteen months later

The photographer checked his light meter, then changed the lens on his camera.

"Renee, please move closer to your husband. Jeremy, you're going to have to hold two of your daughters."

The Blackstones had gathered in Renee and Sheldon's living room for a formal family photo session. In only a year and a half the family had increased by five.

Renee had given birth to a daughter whom she'd named Virginia.

Tricia and Jeremy had become the parents of identical triplet daughters who were feminine miniatures of their father.

Ryan and Kelly had welcomed their third child, a son, who was named for his grandfather, Sheldon James Blackstone the second.

Virginia squirmed to free herself from Renee's arms. "Poppa."

Sheldon reached over and took his daughter, bouncing her on his knee. The chubby little girl had become his pride and joy from the moment she came into the world, crying at the top of her tiny lungs. He'd kissed her, cut the umbilical cord and had claimed her as his own within seconds of her birth. Virginia may have looked like her mother, but there was no doubt she was his daughter.

"Let's do this now," Sheldon ordered the photographer.

The man held up a hand. "One, two, three. Hold it." A flash of light went off, startling the children. They'd barely recovered when another flash followed. This time they laughed, trying to catch the tiny white circles floating in front of their eyes.

The photographer got off one more shot, capturing the lively smiles and bright-eyed stares of the next generation of Virginia Blackstones.

* * * * *

COMING NEXT MONTH

#1651 AWAKEN THE SENSES—Nalini Singh

Dynasties: The Ashtons

Charlotte Ashton was quiet and shy, but to renowned winemaker Alexandre Dupre, she was an intriguing challenge. Charlotte's guarded ways had him wanting to awaken her senses, and pretty soon Alexandre was too tempting to resist. Yet, Charlotte didn't just want a fling—she wanted him forever.

#1652 THE TEMPTING MRS. REILLY—Maureen Child

Three-Way Wager

Brian Reilly had just made a bet not to have sex for three months, when his stunningly sexy ex-wife blew into town. It wasn't long before Tina had him contemplating giving up his wager and getting her back. But the tempting Mrs. Reilly had a reason of her own for wanting Brian to lose his bet…to give her a baby!

#1653 HEART OF THE RAVEN—Susan Crosby

Behind Closed Doors

When private investigator Cassie Miranda was assigned to find a mysterious baby, she never thought she'd have to help out his dashingly handsome father. Reclusive businessman Heath Raven was hardly prepared to become a dad, but Cassie saw a man with a hardened heart that she was all too willing to soothe.

#1654 JARED'S COUNTERFEIT FIANCÉE—Brenda Jackson

When debonair attorney Jared Westmoreland needed a date, he immediately thought of the beautiful Dana Rollins. Reluctantly, Dana fulfilled his request, and the two were somehow stuck pretending that they were engaged! With the passion quickly rising between them, would Jared's faux fiancée turn into the real deal?

#1655 ONLY SKIN DEEP—Cathleen Galitz

To put an end to her single status, Lauren Hewett transformed from shy bookworm into feisty bombshell while her former crush, Travis Banks, watched with more than passing interest. Travis wasn't exactly looking to lay his heart on the line but Lauren wasn't interested in an attraction that was only skin deep….

#1656 BEDROOM SECRETS—Michelle Celmer

Ever since that one time Tyler Douglas had trouble "performing" in the bedroom, he'd been too terrified to even be in the same room with a woman. So when he offered to let the beautiful Tina DeLuca stay in his home, he did all he could to keep her out of his bed. But Ty was more than Tina would—or could—resist….

SDCNM0405